Heinemann
New Windmills

Words Last Forever

From a shocking story about parental rejection to a chilling story of revenge, this collection is gripping and thought-provoking. It explores how words and feelings have the power to change people and situations for better or for worse . . .

About the Author

Malorie Blackman was born in London in 1962 and has spent most of her life there. She has had a variety of jobs including database manager, systems programmer, receptionist and shop assistant.

Malorie's first book, *Not So Stupid!* was published in 1990. After its success she gave up her computing job to become a full-time writer. Since then Malorie has published over forty books and has won a number of awards, including the Young Telegraph Children's Book of the Year Award for *Hacker* (1994) and *Thief!* (1996).

When Malorie isn't writing she enjoys reading and playing her piano and saxophone. She lives in London with her husband and daughter.

MALORIE BLACKMAN

WORDS LAST FOREVER

Heinemann
New Windmills

Heinemann Educational Publishers
Halley Court, Jordan Hill, Oxford OX2 8EJ
A division of Reed Educational and Professional Publishing Ltd

OXFORD MELBOURNE AUCKLAND
JOHANNESBURG BLANTYRE GABORONE
IBADAN PORTSMOUTH (NH) USA CHICAGO

This collection first published in Great Britain 1998 under the title
Words Last Forever by Mammoth, an imprint of Egmont Children's
Books Limited, 239 Kensington High Street, London W8 6SA

This collection © 1999 Oneta Malorie Blackman
Words Last Forever © 1997 Oneta Malorie Blackman
first published in *All for Love*, edited by Miriam Hodgson,
published by Mammoth 1997
Dad, Can I Come Home? © 1990 Oneta Malorie Blackman
first published in *Not So Stupid* by Livewire Books for Teenagers
The author has asserted her moral rights
All rights reserved
This collection first published in the New Windmill Series 2000

04 03 02 01 00
10 9 8 7 6 5 4 3 2 1

ISBN 0 435 12509 5

Cover illustration by Kevin Jenkins
Cover design by The Point
Typeset by ↗ Tek-Art, Croydon, Surrey
Printed and bound in the United Kingdom by Clays Ltd, St Ives plc

Contents

For Neil and Elizabeth
with love

Humming Through My Fingers

My hands slowed down and stilled on my book as I listened. I turned my head and sniffed at the wind. Mum always said I had ears like a bat but if it wasn't for the wind blowing in my direction I doubt if even I would have heard this particular conversation. I listened for a few moments until I'd heard enough, then returned to my book – which was far more interesting. Nine pages on and I was interrupted. I'd thought I'd get at least twelve pages on before he plucked up the nerve to come over.

'Hi, Amber. I'm Kyle. Kyle Bennett.'

I sniffed the air in the direction of the voice. He didn't have to tell me his name. I recognised his voice. Kyle Bennett – the new boy in my brother Jordan's class. Well, when I say new, I mean he'd been in Jordan's class for over a month now. Kyle had been to our house two or three times but this was the first time he'd said anything to me. I sniffed again. I could smell a lie. Not lies. Just one lie. Even if I hadn't heard, I would've known.

'Can I sit down?'

'I don't know.' I shrugged. 'Can you?'

'Huh?'

I smiled. A teeny-tiny smile for a teeny-tiny joke.

'No, I . . . er . . . I meant, d'you mind if I sit down?' Kyle's voice was anxious, eager for me to understand.

'Help yourself.' Why ask me if he could sit down? Did I own the field or the grass in it? I carried on reading my book.

'What're you reading? Is it good?'

Jane Eyre. I've read it before and yes, it is good.'

'If you've read it before, why're you reading it again?' asked Kyle.

'It's one of my favourite books.' All the time I spoke I carried on reading, my fingers skimming over the page. But then my fingers unexpectedly touched Kyle's and an electric shock like summer lightning flashed through my fingers and up my arm.

'Ouch!' Kyle exclaimed.

With his touch still humming through my fingers, I drew my hand away. 'What's the matter?'

'I just got a shock.' Kyle dismissed it easily. I could hear that he was still shaking his sore fingers. 'I don't see how we could've been shocked just sitting on grass.'

I said nothing. It was there in his touch too. The touch of a lie. But there was something else there. Something which stopped me from telling him to put an egg in his shoe and beat it.

'Sorry about that. I just wanted to see what Braille was like.'

'Why?' I could smell his surprise at my question.

'I've never seen a Braille book before. How does it work?'

Here we go again, I sighed. Another explanation. Another embarrassed pause followed by a murmur of sympathy and, under normal circumstances, a sudden mumbled excuse to leave.

'Each of the series of dots represents a letter or a number. I use my fingers to read the dots rather than my eyes to read the words on a page, that's all.'

'Can I have a try?'

'Go ahead.'

I picked up the book, and held it in Kyle's direction. He took it from me, careful not to touch my fingers this time.

'It must take ages to learn all this lot. It would take me years.' Kyle whistled appreciatively. 'How long did it take you?'

2

'Quite a few months.' And I admit, I was surprised. No pity, no sympathy, just two people talking.

'Were you born blind?'

Another surprise. No one ever discussed my eyes – not directly with me at any rate. It was a taboo subject, conspicuous by its absence. I wondered who else was present, who else was listening. I sniffed the air. I couldn't smell anyone else nearby. Just Kyle – and his lie.

'No.' I was going to say more, but the words didn't seem to want to come out of my mouth.

'So, how did you become blind then?'

'I'm a diabetic and I'm one of the unlucky few who became blind because of it.' I faked a shrug.

'What d'you miss most?'

'People's faces – and colours.' Silence stretched between us as I listened to Kyle search for something else to say. This was the crunch moment. 'What would *you* miss most?'

'Pardon?'

I repeated the question and smiled as I heard Kyle frown. 'I don't know,' he answered at last. My question had disturbed him. 'Jordan told me that you see things with your other senses though.'

I didn't reply. Slowly I closed my book and waited.

'He said that you can taste shapes and hear colours.'

Tasting shapes, hearing colours – was that why I'd been singled out by Kyle? Was that all there was to it?

'Is that true?'

I shrugged. I'd have to have a serious word with Jordan when I caught up with him. He wasn't meant to tell anyone about that. It wasn't even his secret to tell, it was my secret. Who else had my brother blabbed to?

'I hope you don't mind me mentioning it. Jordan swore me to secrecy and he hasn't told anyone else – at least that's what he said.'

'Why did he tell you?'

'I don't know. Maybe he thought he could trust me not to tell anyone else.'

I nodded non-committally.

'I've never heard of anything like that before.'

'It's called synaesthesia. About ten people in every million have it so don't go thinking I'm a fruit loop or something.' I couldn't keep the edge out of my voice.

'I didn't think anything of the kind.' Kyle laughed. 'What's it like?'

'What's it like to see using your eyes?'

'It's . . . well, it's . . . it's a bit difficult to explain.'

And I knew he'd got the point. 'Exactly.' Then, wanting to change the subject, I asked, 'So what d'you think of Belling Oak then?'

'It's not bad actually. It's a lot better than my old school. How come you don't come here with your brother?'

Whoosh! Instantly my face flamed, in spite of myself. I turned away, listening to the distant cheers and the shouting as the 100 metres sprint race started.

'I was here for two years but . . . there were problems,' I said, still listening to the race.

'What sort of problems?'

I sighed. I'd say one thing for Kyle, he was persistent. 'If you must know, the teachers spouted on and on about how it would be too dangerous for me, too hazardous, too nerve-wracking, how I'd be teased and bullied – stuff like that.'

'Sounds like excuses to me,' Kyle sniffed.

I turned to face him again. 'It was. I already had friends here and Mum and I kept telling them that I was willing to put up with the rest, but they wouldn't have it. Then they started quoting health and safety regulations at us and they said it would cost too much to have the school converted so that I could find my way around without help. So it didn't happen.'

'Were you very disappointed?'

"Course I was. I'd set my heart on staying at Belling.'
I looked around, seeing it with my memory. All around
me were the acres of grounds, divided by a trickling
stream known as 'The Giggler' because of the sound it
made. I remembered how green the grass was, even in
winter, and how in spring and early summer it was always
covered in daisies. From the classroom windows the
daisies made the grounds look like they were covered in
summer snow. And then there were the tall, sprawling
oaks fringing the stream on both sides. The oaks had
always been my favourite. They whispered amongst
themselves using the wind as cover. At one end of the
upper field was the red brick school building and way
across on the other side, past the lower fields, were the
tennis and netball courts. And the whole thing was so
beautiful. I'd been at Belling for two years before I started
to lose my sight. A whole two years to drink in the sights
and sounds of the place before I got bounced out.

'So where d'you go now?'

'Aranden Hall.'

'Never heard of it.'

'It's a school for the blind. It's about five kilometres
from here.'

I turned back towards the sports field. I was seated
near the stream, under the arms of the huge oak trees
that gave Belling Oak its name. Every sports day, I always
sat in the same spot. Far enough away from everyone else
so that I wouldn't have to worry about being pushed over
or swept aside by overly enthusiastic crowds, but close
enough to hear what was going on. Some of my Belling
friends thought it strange that I should want to sit by
myself for most of the afternoon, but they were used to
me by now. To be honest, I liked my own company. That
and the fact that my friends made me remember . . .
different times. I forced my mind away from those
thoughts to concentrate on the here and now.

5

Jordan my brother was due to run in the 200 metres later on. He'd come last. He always did, but he didn't mind and neither did anyone else. It would've been good to see him run, although my friends said he didn't so much run as plod.

'I'm sorry if I asked too many questions,' said Kyle. 'I didn't mean to upset you.'

'It's OK.' But I didn't deny that he'd upset me. 'Can I ask *you* something?'

I heard him nod, then catch himself and say, 'Yeah! Sure!'

'Why're you over here? I mean, why aren't you with everyone else watching the races?'

Please tell the truth. Please.

'I saw you over here and I just wanted to say hello.'

'I see.' The heat from his lie swept over me like lava.

'Would you . . . er . . . I'm going for a chicken burger after all the events are over. I don't suppose you'd like to come with me?'

Silence stretched between us like a piece of elastic.

'OK,' I said, at last.

'Great! Great!'

'Are you going to go back to your friends and watch the rest of the events?' I asked, still reeling from the relief in his voice.

'No, I thought I'd stay here with you, if that's all right?'

'Sure. Let's go for a walk.'

'A walk?'

'Around the grounds. Away from everyone else.'

'Can you . . . ? I mean, do you want . . . ?'

'I can walk you know.' I laughed. 'It's my eyes that don't work, not my legs.'

'Yeah, of course it is. Sorry.' I heard Kyle get to his feet. I stood up, ignoring the hand he put out to help me.

'Let's walk down stream towards the car park then cross over the stream and walk around the tennis courts,' I suggested.

'Fine.'

We started walking. Kyle stuffed his hands in his pockets.

'So tell me what you can see,' I said.

'Huh?'

'Describe what you can see.' I smiled at Kyle. 'Unless of course, you'd rather not.'

'No, I don't mind. I just . . . OK. Well, we're walking beside the stream now and there are oak trees on either side of the stream and over there is the car park and over there is the school and . . .'

I put my hand on his arm. 'That's not what I meant. Tell me what you can *see*.'

'But I just did.'

I gave him a hard look. 'Kyle, have you got a scarf or a tie or something on you?'

'I've got my school tie on. Why?'

'Is it around your neck?'

'Yes.'

'Take it off and put it around your eyes.'

'Come again?'

'You heard me right the first time.' I laughed.

'Why d'you want me to do that?' Kyle's voice was wary, suspicious.

'I'm going to take you around the grounds.'

'With my eyes blindfolded?'

I laughed at the panic in his voice. 'That's right. You're going to have to trust me.'

'But you . . . you can't see.'

'So I've noticed,' I teased. 'So are you going to do it, or are you going to chicken out?'

Slowly Kyle removed the tie from around his neck and tied it around his eyes.

'You've got to do it so you can't see anything,' I told him.

'I have.'

'No, you haven't.'

'How do you know?' Kyle was amazed. It was very gratifying. 'OK! OK! My eyes are totally covered now.'

'Let me touch your face.'

I heard him lean forward. I ran my fingers lightly over his face. My fingers began to hum again as I touched his skin. He had a large forehead (lots of brains!), a strong nose and a firm chin, and his lips were soft. I couldn't tell about his eyes because they were covered with his tie. His tie smelt of sweet green and sharp, tangy gold. Belling Oak colours. I would've been able to tell the colours even if I didn't already know what they were. Satisfied that his eyes were indeed covered I linked his arm with my own. He instinctively stiffened at that.

'Don't worry, your friends won't be able to see us over here.'

'It's not that,' he lied. 'But suppose we end up in the stream or something?'

'Then we'll get wet!'

There was a pause, then Kyle laughed. His body relaxing he said, 'All right then. D'you know where you're going?'

'I know this school like the back of my hand. Don't worry.'

We walked for a minute, listening to the distant cheers and the occasional birdsong.

'What d'you think of that tree?'

'What tree?'

'The one right in front of us. It's my favourite of all of them here,' I said, adding, 'no, don't,' when I felt his other hand move upwards to remove the tie from around his eyes.

'But I can't see the tree. I can't see anything.'

'See it without using your eyes.'

'How do I do that?'

I took Kyle's hand and stretched it out in front of him until it touched the tree trunk. 'What does it feel like?' I asked.

'Rough.'

'What else?'

'Cool. Sharp in places. Here's a smooth bit.'

'And what does it smell like?'

Kyle looked over towards me.

'Go on!' I encouraged. 'It's national hug-a-tree-trunk day! Tell me what it smells like and feels like.'

Reluctantly Kyle moved in closer to the tree. He stretched out his arms to hold it. I could tell he felt very silly.

'It feels very strong. Like it could be here forever if it was left alone.' Kyle's voice grew more and more quiet, but more and more confident. 'And it's got secrets. It's seen a lot of things and knows a lot of things, but it's not telling. And it smells like . . . like rain and soil and a mixture of things.'

'Come on,' I said, taking his arm again.

'Where're we going?'

'To our next stop.'

I led Kyle further down the stream before I turned us to our left and walked a few steps.

'Now you have to do exactly what I say,' I told him, leading him down a gentle slope.

'Are we going to cross the stream here?' he asked, a frown in his voice.

'That's right.' I smiled. 'We're going to jump across.'

'But . . . but I can't see where I'm going,' Kyle said, aghast.

'Then use your other senses. I'll help you.'

'Why can't we use one of the bridges?'

'Because everyone does that. We're going to be adventurous. I want you to jump from here, like a long jumper. It's less than half a metre to the other side at this point. Just jump, then let your weight fall forward and grab hold of one of the tree roots sticking out of the ground. OK?'

No answer.

'OK, Kyle?'

'D'you really think this is a good idea?'

'Trust me. And once you've grabbed the tree root, haul yourself up out of the way 'cause I'll be right behind you.'

'OK,' Kyle said dubiously.

I straightened him up and said, 'Don't worry. My nan can jump half a metre and she's got bad knees – always assuming I've led us to the right bit of the stream, of course.'

'You mean, you're not sure.' Kyle was appalled.

'I'm only winding you up,' I told him gleefully.

'You're enjoying this, aren't you?'

'You'd better believe it! Now then. After three. One . . . Two . . .'

'Three!' Kyle shouted. And he jumped.

To be honest, I was impressed. I didn't think he had it in him. I heard an 'Ooof!' followed by the mad scramble of his hands as he sought and found a tree root. He hauled himself up the bank to the level ground beyond.

'Here I come.' And I jumped. In a way, I'm sorry Kyle didn't see me. A sighted person couldn't have done it better. I landed cleanly, then stepped up the bank.

'Are you OK?' I asked.

'I think so.'

'How did it feel to jump?'

'I don't know,' said Kyle.

'Yes, you do.'

His sharp intake of breath told me that I was right. 'I was . . . a bit nervous. I know the water is only a few centimetres deep but it suddenly felt like it was kilometres deep and kilometres down.'

'And how did you feel when you landed on the other side?'

'Relieved!'

'Anything else?'

'Yeah. Kind of proud of myself.'

'Being blind is like jumping off a cliff with the water below kilometres deep and kilometres down – except you jump never knowing what's on the other side of the cliff. Everything's an adventure for me. Walking along the street, going into a shop, meeting new people, even reading a book. I never know what I'll come across or what I'll find, whether I'll be delighted or disappointed, hurt or happy. Does that make sense?'

'I think so.' Kyle didn't sound sure at all. But it was enough.

I reached out to link arms with Kyle again. 'Have you still got the tie around your eyes?'

'Yes.'

'Then it's time for our next stop.' I led the way along the fence, past the car park and towards the tennis courts.

'I have no idea where we are,' Kyle said, perplexed.

'That's OK. I do.' We walked on for another few minutes before I stopped.

'Where are we now?' asked Kyle.

'By the tennis courts. What can you hear?'

Kyle was still for a moment. 'Birds and a faint whirring sound.'

'That whirring is the traffic on the other side of the school building.'

Kyle turned his head slightly. 'I can hear some cheering now from the sports field but it's very faint.'

'Anything else?'

'I don't think so.'

'OK. Kneel down.'

'Why?'

'Trust me!'

'Oh dear!' Kyle's tone was dry but he still knelt down.

I smelt what I was looking for. The scent was overwhelming. I took Kyle's hand and put it out to touch the thing I could smell.

'Just use your index finger and your thumb to touch this,' I said.

When Kyle's fingers were on the object I let go of his hand.

'What is it?' he asked, his voice more than curious.

'What d'you think it is?'

'I don't know . . .' Kyle said slowly. 'It feels like a bit of velvet but there wouldn't be velvet around the tennis courts.'

I reached out and touched the object, my fingers next to Kyle's. 'A deep yellow velvet.'

'How can you tell what colour it is?'

'Yellow has got quite a high voice. This yellow's voice is slightly lower which means the shade is deeper but it's definitely yellow.'

'Do you know what it is I'm touching?' Kyle asked.

'Yes, I do.' And all at once I didn't want to do this any more. I felt wistful and sad. 'Take off your tie now. Have a look at what you're touching.'

Kyle removed his tie at once and gasped. 'It's . . . it's a flower . . .' he said, shocked.

'Beautiful, isn't it?'

'A deep yellow flower,' Kyle whispered.

'There's more to seeing than looking, Kyle,' I told him. 'Your eyes work. Never forget what a gift that is. I can taste light and feel colours and I'm grateful. But to *see* . . .'

'A flower . . .' Kyle's voice was awe-struck. I didn't have his full attention. I wondered if he'd even heard me.

'Kyle, touching that flower and seeing it with your fingers – that's what seeing with my other senses is a tiny bit like. I see things in ways that you can't or won't because you don't have to. I'm grateful for that as well. Because I can still appreciate the things around me. Maybe even more than a lot of sighted people do.'

I sensed Kyle looking at me then. Really looking – for the first time. I wondered how he saw me now. I smiled at him.

'I . . . look, I have to tell you something,' Kyle began uneasily.

'Forget it.'

'No, it's important. I . . .'

'Dean and Joseph bet you that you couldn't get me to go out for a burger with you. But for your information, they've each asked me out and I turned them down flat, so they reckoned you had no chance.'

Silence.

'Stop it! You're staring!' I laughed.

'How did you know that?'

'What? About the bet or that you were staring?'

'Both.'

''Cause I'm special!' I teased. 'And by the way, I wouldn't tell my brother about the bet if I were you. He's a bit over-protective where I'm concerned and he'd probably want to punch your lights out.'

'I . . . I suppose you don't want anything more to do with me?'

'I knew about the bet before you'd even said one word to me – remember?'

'I still don't understand how.'

'I heard you.'

'But we were practically across the field,' Kyle protested.

'No, you weren't. You were only several metres away and the wind was blowing in my direction.' When Kyle didn't answer I said, 'I have ears like a bat.'

'We'd better get back,' Kyle said, his tone strange.

Now it was my turn to be surprised. 'What's the matter?'

It was a long time before Kyle answered. We started back to the sports field, my arm lightly resting on his. I knew the way back without any problems but I wanted to sense what he was feeling. And it didn't take a genius to guess from the way his muscles were stiff and tense what was going on in his head. He wasn't happy.

'Kyle?'

'I'm sorry, Amber. I guess you hate me now. I don't blame you. I behaved like a real moron.' The words came out in a rush of genuine embarrassment. And there was something else, something more behind them.

'Why should I hate you?'

He looked at me then. And his eyes hadn't changed back – I could tell. He was still looking at me with the eyes of someone who could see *me*. Not a blind girl. Not someone to be pitied or patronised. Not someone who had less than him. But a girl who could see without using her eyes.

'So, d'you still want to go out for a burger?' Kyle's voice was barely above a whisper. If it wasn't for my bat ears I doubt if I would've heard him.

''Course. I'm starving.'

There was no mistaking the sigh of relief that came from Kyle. It made me giggle.

'D'you know something?' Kyle stopped walking. He looked all around him, then straight at me. 'I hadn't noticed before, but everything around me is . . .'

He shut up then. I could feel the self-conscious waves of heat radiating from him. I couldn't help it. I burst out laughing, which made Kyle even more self-conscious.

'Come on,' I said. 'Let's go and watch my brother come last in the four by one-hundred relay.'

And we walked over the bridge together to join the others.

Dad, Can I Come Home?

'Dad? Dad! It's Eve. How are you? What are you doing with yourself? Are you all right?'

'Eve? Eve darling, how are you? It's so good to hear your voice. Where are you? Why can't I see you?'

'Dad, the screen of this video-phone isn't working. And the fleet's just returned to Tdir-ah so the queues to use the phones are *ginormous*. It was use this phone or wait another week to find a phone with a working screen.'

'No, no, it's enough just hearing your voice, bunny. Are you all right?'

'I'm fine, Dad.' Eve smiled again, stretching out a tentative arm to the blank screen before her. 'I've missed you so much. I just can't wait to get home.'

'So the reports are true? The war *is* finally over?'

'The war's over. The treaty was ratified three days ago. I should be home within the week, if the shuttle bus doesn't give up under the strain.'

'Bunny, that's great news. Wait till I tell Joe and Luke, and especially Morgan – eh!'

Eve's cheeks burned. 'Dad, stop teasing! Besides, Morgan is probably married with eight kids by now.'

'Of course he's not married. He's waiting for you. Mind you, if you told him that, he'd laugh in your face but it's the truth.'

'Is it, Dad? Is it really?'

''Course it is.'

'Listen, Dad. I can't stay on the phone for much longer. There's a time limit on all comms to Earth until further notice. I . . . I wanted to ask you for a favour though.'

'Go ahead, bunny.'

Eve swallowed hard. 'You've met Janice my co-pilot. Did you like her?'

'Yes, of course I did.' Eve heard the surprise in her father's voice. She ran her dry tongue over her lips.

'It's just that . . . well, we were shot down over Zitunm . . .'

'WHAT! You didn't tell me that . . . are you sure you're . . .'

'I'm fine,' Eve interrupted. 'But Janice . . . but Janice isn't, Dad. She was thrown clear but she went back to get me. She saved my life.'

'So what's the matter with her?'

'She . . . she was shot dragging me clear. Shot with a senso-blaster.'

'Oh no . . .'

'Exactly, she's lost an arm and both of her legs and her face is severely burnt – almost beyond recognition. And she's not eligible for artificial limbs because she broke the rules by going back for me. I know those artificial limbs aren't much use but at least they're better than the nothing she's going to get because of me.'

'Oh my God. That poor, poor kid.'

Silence.

'Eve? What's the matter, bunny?'

'Sorry, Dad, I was just thinking.' Eve forced herself to continue, 'Janice smiles a lot but deep down she feels very scared, and very alone. She has no family – no one to go back to. So I said that she could stay with us.'

'Stay with us? For how long?'

'For good.'

Eve listened to the silence that filled the video-phone booth. The unspoken plea reverberating through her mind deafened her.

16

'Eve darling, maybe Janice can stay for a day or two, or perhaps even a week, but no way can she live with us permanently.'

'Why not?'

'Eve, use your head. I'll always be grateful to Janice for saving your life. Always. But we have to face the facts. Janice is a cripple . . . she'll need a lot of time and attention. She'll require a lot of care, not to mention money. Our home is too small to have her here permanently and it would cost too much to adapt it.'

'But, Dad, she saved my life. Couldn't we at least try? She wouldn't be too much trouble . . .'

'Yes she would, darling. Don't you think I'd love to say yes but I can't. Maybe she could go into a hospital for the war wounded and we could visit her?'

'She'd hate that. *Please*, Dad . . .'

'I'm sorry, bunny, but the answer is no.'

'But I've already told her she could live with us.'

'Then you'll just have to untell her.'

'Couldn't we just try, Dad. *Please*, for me?'

'No, Eve. She saved your life and I'll always – *always* be grateful for that but she'd be too much of a burden.'

'Burden?' Eve whispered.

'I'm sorry, Eve.'

Silence.

'Come on, Eve. Let's not argue. I haven't spoken to you in over two years. Tell me all about . . .'

'I can't, Dad. My time's up now.'

'Already?'

''Fraid so. I'll see you soon. Bye, Dad. I love you.'

'I love you too, bunny. I'm going to give you such a homecoming. And Eve. I'm sorry about Janice, but you do understand . . . ?'

'I understand, Dad. Bye.'

'Bye, darling. See you soon.'

Eve switched off the video-phone. She stared up at the peeling, dingy grey paint on the ceiling of the booth . . . and cried.

'Mr Walker, it's Janice Sonderguard here.'

'Janice? Well, hello, Janice. How are you?'

'I'm all right, Mr Walker.' Janice studied the image of Eve's father on the phone. He was just as she remembered, his hair grey at his temples but jet everywhere else. A neat, trim moustache and his skin the colour of oak, his body as sturdy as oak. And smiling eyes. A man you instinctively trusted. Solid, dependable. Only he was frowning now.

'Why, Janice, Eve told me that you'd lost an arm and your legs. Have the rules been relaxed? Have you received replacements after all?' Janice turned away from the screen, her lips a tight, bitter line. It didn't matter what the politicians and the diplomats said, the war wasn't over . . . not by *any* means.

'Congratulations. Eve must be so pleased for you.'

Janice turned back to the screen, staring at Mr Walker's broad grin.

'Mr Walker, *please*.' Janice hugged her arms around her body before dropping them to her sides. 'Mr Walker, please prepare yourself. I . . . I've got some bad news.'

'Eve,' Mr Walker said immediately. 'What's wrong? Has something happened to Eve?'

'Mr Walker, I don't know how to say this. Eve . . . Eve committed suicide this morning. I . . . I . . .' The man and woman stared at each other.

'Eve . . . ?' Mr Walker whispered. 'She didn't . . . she wouldn't . . . What are you talking about?'

'*Please*, Mr Walker, I'm telling you the truth. She's dead,' Janice shouted back. 'She's dead,' she whispered.

'But why? WHY? I don't understand.' Janice jumped as Mr Walker punched the screen. 'Why are you doing this to me? Why?'

'Mr Walker, Eve spoke to you last night. Did you see her? What did she talk about?'

'What . . . ?' Mr Walker shook his head slowly, utterly bewildered now, utterly lost. 'I can't . . . I . . . never saw her yesterday. The screen in the video-phone booth wasn't working . . . She talked about you, she wanted you to stay with us.'

'Me?' Janice said slowly.

'She told me that you'd lost an arm and both legs –'

'Oh I see,' Janice whispered.

'I don't understand,' Mr Walker pleaded.

'Eve left you a letter. Can I read it to you?'

Mr Walker nodded slowly.

Janice removed the letter from her overall pocket. There was sand in her throat, threatening to choke her as she began to read:

Sorry Dad. I love you. You've explained everything to me very carefully and I think this is the best solution for everyone.

'What does that mean?' Mr Walker interrupted. 'Eve *can't* be dead . . . I don't believe it.'

'Mr Walker, let me show you Eve. She's . . . in the morgue. I can transmit the image to you.'

'I don't understand any of this . . .'

Janice keyed the necessary commands into the console beside the video-phone and the morgue appeared without warning, filled to overflowing with row upon row of body capsules. Janice began to key in the commands to home in on the appropriate capsule.

'Mr Walker, did Eve tell you about our crash on Zitunm?'

'Yes, she told me how you saved her life.'

'I didn't save *her* life, Mr Walker,' Janice said quietly. 'It was the other way around. She came back for me . . .'

A new image filled the screen now. There in her capsule lay Eve Walker, Captain of the SAXICON ship, with no legs and only one arm and a badly scarred, almost unrecognisable face.

Matt Ludlum

I loved Matt Ludlum. He had what my big sister called 'dew-drop' lips and twinkling eyes and a shapely haircut. He was a cousin of Claudette and Jackson Sullivan next door and he lived in Richmond. That's practically all I knew about him but it didn't matter, because I loved him.

And then my chance came. The Sullivans were going to see his family and Mr Sullivan invited me along.

'Yes, please,' I said, snatching his hand off.

I'd only seen Matt five or six times, but I truly loved him. I *dreamt* about him. Every night I practised kissing my pillow, pretending it was Matt. I'd tilt my head to the left, then to the right – trying to find the position that felt the most comfortable, the most natural. I even looked up kissing in our encyclopaedias just to get some hints, but that was a dead loss. I wanted to be *ready*. If . . . no, *when* Matt kissed me. I wanted him to think that I kissed boys all the time. No foreheads bumping, no noses thumping. Just lips meeting.

The trouble was whenever Matt and I were together, my family and the Sullivans teased us so mercilessly that Matt had barely said two sentences to me the last time we'd met. But as Ellen, my older sister, pointed out, 'If he didn't fancy you, he wouldn't be bothered about the teasing, now would he?'

I don't know if Ellen was just saying that to be kind – actually, thinking about it, Ellen is never kind to me, so she must have been telling the truth – or else she was on a wind up. I chose to believe that she was right and he did fancy me.

Anyway, the big day arrived. I was off to Richmond to see Matt Ludlum. I got into the back of Mr Sullivan's van with Claudette and Jackson, the Sullivan crew, and at last we were off. Ellen cried off with a make-believe migraine. I spent most of the journey staring out of the window, trying to memorise the route so I'd be able to find my way back to Matt on my own. Within minutes I didn't know where we were but that didn't matter. I kept my eyes open for unusual landmarks, things to remember for my journey back to him.

When we finally reached Matt's house, my heart was pounding. Would Matt be as glad to see me as I was to see him? Of course he would be! After all, I loved him. But when we walked into the Ludlum's living-room, Matt took one look at me and said coldly, 'What's she doing here? Who invited her?'

'Matt, boy, what's happened to your manners?' his mother asked, more surprised than anything else.

Matt just frowned and looked away from me. But I didn't care. He was a boy so he couldn't very well show that he was actually *glad* to see me. After we had all eaten, Mr Ludlum suggested that us kids go to the park to play rounders. We walked to the park in pairs and somehow, some lucky how, Matt walked beside *me*.

'What school d'you go to?' he asked.

I looked down at the pavement as if I'd never seen it before. 'Chesterfield Girls. It's a grammar school.' The moment it was out, I could've bitten off my tongue. I gritted my teeth, agonised. Would he think I was boasting? I wasn't, I really wasn't. Was he the type of boy who liked his girlfriends to have a few brain cells to rub together? Or was he the sort who liked his girlfriends to look good but have nothing to say for themselves? Boys were so difficult!

'Which school do you go to?' I asked. Keep the conversation going, Hilary, I thought, trying not to panic. You don't want him to think that you're boring.

'Lenwood *Secondary*,' he stressed.

My face burnt hot. I wasn't trying to pose or imply anything by saying that I went to a grammar school but Matt obviously thought otherwise.

'What . . . what are you going to do when you leave school?' I rushed on.

'I don't know,' Matt said coldly. 'Maybe go to university.'

'To do what?'

'I don't . . .'

'Look at those two lovebirds,' Claudette called from behind us.

Matt instantly moved further away from me. I gave Claudette a filthy look. Stupid cow! I thought miserably. And I'd been doing so well.

At the park, Claudette organised us into two teams of three. I was on one side with Beverley and Teddy – Matt's brother and sister – whilst Matt was on the other side with Jackson and Claudette. Our side was put in to bat first. Matt was bowling. I couldn't wait to stand opposite him. I was quite good at rounders. I couldn't throw the ball to save my life but I could hit it and catch it. I'd show him that I was all right – for a girl! I was the second one in our team to bat. I stood behind Jackson Sullivan's coat which marked the batting area. I prayed that I would hit the ball out of the park and get a rounder. Then Matt would be impressed. He would see I was super-fit, well co-ordinated and able to hold a reasonably decent conversation. Next time though, I'd look him straight in the eyes as he spoke to me, not down at the pavement. Then he would love me. By the time I'd finished with him, he'd be like ice cream in my hands!

Matt bowled deliberately fast. Not even blinking, my eyes tracked the ball's path as it hurtled towards me. I swung at the ball, my energy focused on my right arm. BOCK! The ball speared through the air between the third and

*fourth bases. I was at first base, now second . . .
Jackson Sullivan, racing like the devil was chasing him,
ran after the ball as it sped across the ground. He
scooped it up and threw it. Third base . . . Who would
reach fourth base first – the ball or me? I threw myself
past the jacket that was fourth base just as Claudette
caught the ball.*

Close, but no contest!

*Gulping down air whilst my team cheered for me,
I looked at Matt. He smiled. I smiled. He clapped slowly,
sincerely.*

'Well done, Hilary,' he said.

'Thanks!' I breathed.

*He was definitely impressed. Maybe I could put all
that kissing practice performed with my pillow to some
good use later . . .*

Matt bowled deliberately fast. Not even blinking, my eyes
tracked the ball's path as it hurtled towards me. I swung
the bat and missed, giving the air a good wallop. The ball
flew on to hit me full on the nose. I dropped my bat and
started bawling. How could Matt be so nasty? Especially
when I loved him? My nose started to bleed. Drops of
blood splattered on my white T-shirt. I tilted my head
forward and went on sobbing – in between swallowing
my blood. Everyone rushed over to me. Beverley, Matt's
sister, gave me some grubby tissues from her trouser
pockets. I pinched my nose and looked at Matt.

'I'm sorry, I'm sorry,' Matt said quickly.

We all walked back home. Rounders was over.

'You're for it now, Matt,' Teddy kept saying.

Soon they were all at it.

'You are in so much trouble.'

'No more pocket money for a year.'

'No dinner for you tonight.'

'Straight to bed *and* you'll miss the horror film.'

They went on and on and on. How I wished they'd all shut up and leave him alone. Then without warning Matt burst into tears.

'Don't cry, Matt,' I said, still pinching my nose. 'Please don't cry.'

I tried my best to placate him but it didn't help. My nose went on bleeding, Matt went on crying. The others kept on teasing him until, by the time we got back, my head as well as my nose was hurting. No sooner had we set foot in Matt's house when his mum and dad appeared, followed by Mr and Mrs Sullivan.

'What happened?' Matt's mum looked at me, shocked.

'I fell over and my nose started bleeding,' I said before anyone else could speak.

Matt's dad frowned. 'Why're you crying, boy?'

Matt sniffed and said nothing. No one else said a word either.

'Can I use your bathroom please?' I said to Matt's mum.

'Of course. Come, I'll take you.' Matt's mum put one hand on my shoulder and led the way upstairs. Halfway up the stairs I turned to look at Matt. He looked straight up at me. Then he looked down at the carpet.

We had dinner and played Monopoly until Mr Sullivan announced that it was time to go home. I looked across at Matt but he didn't look back at me. Since the walk home from the park, he hadn't said one word to me. I'd tried to talk to him all evening but he didn't just ignore me, he treated me as if I didn't exist. Slowly I realised that somehow I had hurt his pride. He'd cried in front of his family and relations and worst of all, he'd cried in front of me. He'd never forgive me for that.

And I was right. Matt never spoke to me again.

Snippets of Mum

I sat at the top of the wall bars staring at the PE mat on the hard parquet floor three metres beneath me.

Jump, Jade! Come on! Jump!

One more year, just one more year. Then I'd be old enough to leave school. I could get a job, get my own flat and most important of all – *I could leave home*. I had to get out before Mum drove me crazy. I couldn't do anything right – not ever. All she did was nag, nag, nag.

'Jade, have you done your homework; Jade, have you done the housework; you can't go out; you're so lazy; Jade, take that muck off your face; Jade; JADE; JADE!'

Nag, nag, nag. On and on and on. Why didn't I just run away? I wished I could. I wished I had the guts.

Jump, Jade.

I looked down at the floor again. I'd done this hundreds of times, so why hesitate?

Get on with it! Jump, Jade.

Mum's angry face appeared in my head against my will. I remembered last night's argument. It could've been last week's or last month's. All Mum and I ever did was argue.

'I hate it here. I hate everything about it. And I hate you.'

'Stop being stupid, Jade. You're lucky we have somewhere to live at all,' Mum shouted.

I looked around, full of loathing for the dung-heap the council had deigned to give us.

'This isn't a house, it's a dump. It's worse than a dump. I hate it. And it's all your fault.' If Mum could shout loudly, then I could shout louder.

'How is it my fault? Your father ran off and left us and the bank repossessed the house a week later. If I hadn't spent months and months sitting in the housing office at the council, we wouldn't even have this much. So how exactly is it all my fault?'

'I hate you.'

'And you make me sick, so that makes us even,' Mum said bitterly.

Come on, Jade, Jump.

I took a deep breath – and I jumped.

The instant my feet touched the ground, a shock like lightning shot up both legs. I froze. But the shock was gone almost as suddenly as it had arrived.

'Jade, you know better than that,' Miss Frost shouted from across the hall. 'The next time you jump, bend your legs to absorb the impact.'

'Yes, miss,' I called back. And I ran forward to the next piece of apparatus, the low benches. It was time to pretend I was a world-class gymnast at the Olympics and on my favourite piece of apparatus – the beam!

'What's the matter with you, Jade?'

'I jumped off the wall bars in PE today,' I said through gritted teeth. 'And I think I've done something to my legs.'

'Do you want me to call the doctor?'

'It's too late now.' I stood in front of the paraffin heater, holding up the back of my dress to above my waist. The heat seemed to help, just.

'I'll get your dinner.'

'No, Mum. I'm not hungry. You have it. I think I'll go to bed.'

Mum looked at me, worried. 'If you're not better tomorrow, I'll go round the corner to the phone box and call out the doctor.'

It took me ten minutes to get up the stairs. I went straight to bed without even cleaning my teeth. I was burning hot and burning cold and I felt sick.

Just get a good night's sleep and you'll feel fine in the morning, I told myself. I closed my eyes and forced myself to fade out.

The next morning, I woke up and flung back my blanket. I tried to sit up but my body felt strange. I couldn't move my legs. Not one centimetre. I couldn't get up. Terrified, I started screaming.

'Mum! Mum!' I didn't stop yelling for her until she came running into the room.

'What is it? What's the matter?'

'I can't move my legs, Mum. They hurt. They hurt so much.'

Mum sat down on the bed.

'Don't bounce on the bed,' I shrieked at her. 'It hurts.'

She took my hand. 'I'm going to call the doctor, Jade. I'll have to go to the telephone box around the corner but I'll be right back.'

I hardly heard her. 'What's wrong with my legs, Mum?' I cried. Tears ran into my ears and the pillow beneath my head was soaked.

'I'll be right back, Jade.'

'WHAT'S THE MATTER WITH MY LEGS?' I couldn't focus on anything but the pain in my legs and the fact that I couldn't move them.

What had I done?

'Do you want some Horlicks before the doctor comes?' Mum asked.

'Yes, please.'

'He won't be long now, dear.' She smiled down at me.

Mum left the room, returning a few minutes later with a steaming cup in her hand.

'Here, drink this.' Mum sat down very tentatively at the edge of the bed.

'I can't sit up,' I complained.

'I'll hold you up with one arm and hold the cup with the other,' Mum suggested. She got up very slowly, each action definite and controlled. Then she sat down by my head, again taking her time over every movement. She placed the cup on the floor before helping me to sit up. It was a slow, painful process. Neither of us said a word until I was sitting up and leaning against the wall behind me.

'Drink this whilst it's hot. It'll bring the wind out of your stomach,' said Mum.

'It's not my stomach I'm worried about.'

We both smiled. Mum fed me the Horlicks, allowing me to take my time. I had just finished drinking when there was a knock at the front door. Mum leapt off the bed and I screamed with pain.

'Oh, I'm sorry, Jade. I'm sorry.' Mum gave me an agonised look before rushing to answer the door.

Moments later the doctor entered the bedroom. He gave me a thorough examination, asking me a lot of questions at the same time. Finally he stood up straight and scratched his bald head.

'It's more painful than serious,' he told Mum. 'She's sprained both of her legs quite badly but as there's no longer any fever there's no need for Jade to go to hospital.' He leant against the tall chest of drawers to write out the prescription. 'This is for some cream which you'll have to rub into her legs three times a day and some tablets she should take three times a day about an hour before each meal.'

'How long before she's on her feet again?' Mum asked.

The doctor shook his head. 'Three to four weeks I'm afraid. But after that she'll be as good as new.'

Once the doctor had left, Mum said, 'I'll take this to the chemist now. I'll be right back.'

'But the local chemist isn't open today.'

'I'll go into town for it. I'll be back as soon as I can.'

An hour and a half later, Mum was back. She took off her coat, flung it over the chair before the bay window and threw back the bedclothes before applying liberal amounts of the huge tube of cream to each leg. It felt cold and sticky. Mum spent ten minutes rubbing the cream into each leg. We didn't speak. Then she made my favourite meal for lunch – cod-in-butter sauce, a cheese, onion and potato pie and garden peas. And I had a whole can of ginger beer to myself. Mum spent the next three weeks running up and down the stairs after me. And we talked. She talked and I listened. And to my amazement, I realised I didn't know her. I didn't know her at all.

'Where were you born, Mum?'

'Barbados.'

'I know that,' I sniffed. 'Where abouts?'

'Millervale, St Andrews.'

'I already know that . . .'

'Then you know as much as I do. I was born at home in Millervale, St Andrews,' Mum said, exasperated.

'What was it like?'

'Warmer! Warmer than here. But the funny thing is, I can't take the heat in this country.'

'Why not?' I laughed. 'Heat is heat. There's only one sun shining on us.'

'Ah, but it's not the same. In Barbados, there's always a cool breeze off the sea. In this country it's too humid and sticky. You just sweat and don't want to do anything. They can't get anything right in this country.'

And at that we both roared with laughter.

'So how many houses *have* you lived in?' I asked.

'I've lost count.' Mum continued to slowly rub the cream into my legs. 'I've lived in Stoke Newington,

Islington, New Cross – that was when you were born. The landlady we had at the time said to me, "Pearl, if it wasn't for Jade, I would ask you and your husband to leave."' Mum shook her head at the memory.

'Why did she want to chuck you out?'

'Jade, your father didn't like to pay his rent. That's why I always make sure my rent gets paid now, even if I don't eat . . . Where was I? Oh yes! We've lived in Peckham, Morden, Merton, Harlesden, Deptford, Catford, Lewisham, Sydenham, Beckenham, Forest Hill, Tottenham, Fulham – I didn't like Fulham at all – Hammersmith . . .'

'Bloomin' heck, Mum. Is there anywhere in London you haven't lived?'

'Don't swear, Jade, it's common. And in answer to your question, no, I don't think there is. I've lived in every London borough there is at least once. And every time I'd just settled, we'd be up and flying away from some landlord or bank or building society. That man didn't like to pay his rent for a joke!'

I remembered the last place we had all lived in together, before Dad did his sunlight sprint and the bailiffs had chucked us out. I remembered Dad showing us around and Mum standing stiff as a board in the hall, refusing to show any interest.

Dad hit the roof at that. But I understood now. We were just looking around another temporary bolthole as far as Mum was concerned. Now Mum was smiling at me. I couldn't smile back.

'When your nan and I first came over to this country, we went to church in . . .' Mum pondered for a moment. 'In Morden or Merton or one of those places. I'll never forget it. When the pastor had finished his dry preaching, everyone in our row used to stand up and rush past us before we could move. They'd purposely brush against

31

us, moving their hands quickly over our hands and forearms.' Mum laughed at the thought.

'Why'd they do that?'

'To see if our colour came off.'

'You're joking!'

'I'm not, you know.'

'How old were you?'

'Six or seven.'

'Did you know what they were doing – all those ones who kept touching you?' I asked.

'I asked my mum but she didn't answer. But it didn't take long for me to work it out for myself.'

I couldn't speak. I just stared at her.

'Jade, don't worry about it. It was a long, long time ago.'

'I guess so. I mean, you are ancient.'

'Thanks a lot!'

'But even so, forty odd years ago isn't that far back. I mean we're not talking about Victorian times are we?'

I had a lot to think about.

'I remember when that wretch Shaun Weston spat at you . . .' Mum's face clouded over as she spoke.

All at once the memory was as clear and sharp as if it had only just happened. Shaun Weston spat at me and he and his two friends laughed as I burst into tears. I cried all the way home. Cried until my whole body hiccuped.

'You marched along the high street in your curlers and apron with your slippers still on your feet. I was so embarrassed,' I smiled.

'I didn't care. I was ready to put that boy over my knee and slap his backside until it burnt my hand!'

'I know you were.'

'Damn boy! His mother needed a good slap too. Telling me that he didn't mean to do it. I suppose the spit just leapt spontaneously from his mouth.'

'Calm down, Mum.'

'And I suppose it had nothing to do with him?'
'Calm down! That was years ago.'
'It still makes me mad. Damn boy. Hhmm!'
'Don't swear, Mum. It's common!'

'Jade, aren't you a bit old to be still sucking your tongue!'
'I wasn't . . .'
'You were . . .'
'I wasn't . . .'
'You were . . .'
And we both creased up laughing.

'What would you do if Dad came back?' I asked.
'I don't know.' Mum shrugged. 'Everything would be fine for six months or so and then I'd be right back where I started. It always works that way. So I don't know.'
I watched her and wondered how she couldn't know. After everything Dad had put her through? If it was me, he wouldn't get a foot in the door. Did Mum still love Dad?

'Snap!'
'They're not the same, Mum.'
'Oh yes,' Mum said, absent-mindedly.
I shook my head. Honestly. 'Concentrate, Mum. Concentrate.'
'My mind isn't on this.'
'I would never have guessed!'

'I didn't know you could play the piano!' Mum was playing *There Is A Green Hill Far Away* on the keyboard Dad bought for me two birthdays ago. She was good! Very good.
'I've always had a good ear for music.'
'I didn't know that.'
'I know you didn't,' Mum winked.

*

And Mum rubbed my legs, three times a day, day in day out. I looked at her as she frowned with concentration.

My mother . . . Pearl Davies née Atwood. My mum. A woman separated from her husband. A woman surviving. I remembered when I was seven or eight the amazement I felt when I learnt that Mum's name wasn't Mum but Pearl. Mum lifted her head and looked at me. We smiled.

'I wanted to stay on at school but Ma and Pa couldn't afford it. So I left when I was fourteen and became an apprentice to a seamstress. Her name was Ophelia. That's where I got your middle name from. Well, from there and Shakespeare! Ophelia was a good teacher and a good friend, and *Hamlet* was always my favourite Shakespeare play. So I got two for the price of one.'

Up until that moment, I'd always hated my middle name.

'I didn't know you did Shakespeare at school,' I said, aghast.

'What did you think we did?' Mum said loftily. 'We also did *The Odyssey* by Homer . . .'

'You're joking!' I was even more astounded.

'And we did French – *la chaise, la table, le lit* . . .' Mum pointed to the chair, the table, the bed.

I stared until my eyes were ready to pop out of my head and plop into my lap.

'And calculus and Milton . . .' Mum continued.

'I'm doing Milton,' I said, excitedly. '*Paradise Lost.*'

'We did the first four books of that.'

'We're only doing the first two.'

'You see, I'm not stupid. Your mother isn't stupid.'

'Yes, I do see,' I said slowly. And it was as if I was really seeing for the first time. Even if Mum hadn't done all those things, she still wouldn't be stupid. She'd done so much, been through so much, knew so much. There were wells of common sense in her, stores of experience that I hadn't even guessed at.

34

I was ashamed. When Dad was around I'd listened to his tales of how stupid Mum was. Worse still I'd believed them. I hadn't seen that Dad was all bluff and bluster, whereas Mum was a silent star – knowing what she was worth without having to force the fact upon anyone else. Here I was, Jade Ophelia Davies, and it was a real eye-opener to learn I was nowhere near as perceptive as I'd always imagined.

In the third week of my stay off school, Mum was rubbing some cream into my legs when she suddenly said, 'Do you know something, Jade? You're not so bad after all.'

'I was thinking exactly the same thing about you. You're not so bad either.'

And we started laughing.

Suddenly, I didn't want to get well. I didn't want to lose my newly-found mum.

The following week, when I was finally back on my feet, we were a bit wary of each other for a couple of days. I think we both feared the same thing – that things would go back to the way they were before my accident. But we weren't just mother and daughter any more, we were friends. Good friends. Best friends.

So this story is for my mum, Pearl Atwood Davies – a bright, right, light shining star. Not because I love her very much – which I do, but because I *like* her. And there's nothing written that says you have to *like* your parents.

The Turning Point

'Jungle bunny . . . cannibal . . .'

Graeme put his hands over his ears but the hateful, hurtful words still echoed around him. Lightning flashed, momentarily turning the dark sky a pale grey. It was immediately followed by a raging roar of thunder overhead – but even that could not obliterate the taunts directed at him.

'Cannibal!'

The rain poured. Graeme wiped his face but it made no difference. His cheeks, his eyes, his lips, they were all wet.

'Cannibal . . . rotten, stinking cannibal . . .'

Graeme dropped his hands, surreptitiously feeling behind him. His hands immediately met with a brick wall. No escape that way then.

He glared at the four boys before him. Matthew – tall with blond hair down to his shoulders. He followed the others like a sheep. Lucas – small and pudgy, with a body shaped like a rugby ball. He'd run a mile if he was on his own and saw Graeme, but Lucas felt safe with the other bullying cowards. Then there was Toto – the Japanese boy who, when he had arrived in Britain two years ago, couldn't speak a word of English.

And then there was Jude. Jude, who had been in Graeme's class since infant school. Jude, who had been Graeme's best friend until about a year and a half ago. In fact, they were more than best friends. As far as Graeme was concerned they were more like brothers. But then Jude's dad had remarried and Jude's stepmum – what was the phrase Jude had used then? – Jude's stepmum had some *strange* ideas. Jude told Graeme some of them.

'The holocaust didn't really happen. It's just Jewish propaganda . . . Black people,' (only she hadn't used that phrase) 'are the lowest of the low and it's God's will that they remain that way.'

Graeme wondered why on earth Jude's dad had married such a poisonous troll. And as for Jude? Well, he just laughed at his stepmum at first. Graeme didn't laugh. Jude's new mum sounded dangerous and Graeme worried about what she might do to Jude.

But what had happened was worse than Graeme ever imagined. Jude started listening to her. And the more he listened, the less he wanted to be with Graeme. Graeme still couldn't believe how slow he'd been to recognise what was going on – the silences, the strange, speculative looks, the offhand manner, the excuses made whenever Graeme suggested they do something together. It took a while but Graeme finally got the message.

And over the last eighteen months, Graeme could do nothing but watch as Jude slowly but surely grew to hate him. Try as he might, Graeme just couldn't understand it. He and Jude had been friends for such a long time and Jude had known his new mum for such a short time. Was it really just his new mum spewing venom that had changed Jude so much? Was that really all it took?

Graeme had lain in bed, staring up at the ceiling many nights, trying to put his finger on the turning point. Only now did Graeme realise that there was no action, no phrase which had turned Jude vicious – at least, none perpetrated by him.

'Cannibal . . .'

Graeme inhaled deeply, sucking in the last of his courage before it fled. He tried to walk through the mob. They pushed him back against the wall.

'Where d'you think you're going?' Jude sneered.

Graeme remained silent. He knew from past experience that anything he said would just make matters worse. If only it was one against one, even one against two, then he might stand a chance. But one against four . . . He'd be hammered into the ground.

Graeme stared at Jude, not attempting to hide or even disguise what he thought, what he felt. Jude's eyes narrowed. Graeme knew what was coming next. This time I'll fight back, Graeme thought, tensing his muscles, clenching his fists. Even if I lose, I'll fight back.

In the distance, Graeme spotted Mrs Gowers heading for the school gates. He willed the teacher to turn around and look at him, to see what was going on. He stared at her, barely daring to blink. The teacher stopped walking, a frown on her face. Graeme stared harder. He took a step towards her. Mrs Gowers turned her head, just as Jude shoved Graeme back against the wall.

She hurried on. Hadn't she seen him?

Graeme tried to concentrate on her again but Jude and the others moved to stand in his way so he could no longer see her. Jude and his friends stood so close to Graeme that he couldn't even raise his arm to wipe the rainwater out of his eyes.

There came a sudden flash of lightning, so bright that the light hurt Graeme's eyes. A swift punch to his stomach and Graeme doubled over, coughing hard, trying desperately to catch his breath. Then something hard and heavy hit Graeme's head, followed by a pounding in his ears. An instant later inky blackness swallowed Graeme whole as he fell insensible to the ground.

Graeme opened his eyes, instantly awake. He saw a custard-coloured ceiling which he didn't recognise. Turning his head, Graeme looked around.

38

'Graeme, love, are you all right?'

'Mum? Where am I? What happened?'

'You were hit on the head. You're in hospital.' His mum's face was directly above him, twisting first with relief, then fear. 'You've had a very lucky escape. Your guardian angel must have been in your pocket when the bricks hit you.'

'Bricks?'

'A couple of them got dislodged from the wall behind you and fell,' Mum explained. 'It must've been the storm that did it.'

'Who told you that?'

'Isn't that what happened?'

Graeme frowned. That's not how he remembered it – at all. He threw back the crocheted blanket which covered him. He held up his hands to the light. He looked down at his body.

'Am I all right?' he asked.

'You're fine. Like I said, you had a lucky escape. How do you feel?'

'Not bad,' Graeme said slowly.

That was a lie. He felt good. In fact he felt great – never better.

'Ah, Graeme.' A woman doctor drew back the riotously coloured curtain which made up the cubicle walls. 'I'm Doctor Cardie. How are you?'

'Fine.' Graeme sat up quickly. 'Can I go home now?'

The doctor smiled. 'You have to stay in overnight in case of a possible concussion.'

'But I'm all right.'

'Well, I've just got one or two more tests to carry out, then we'll see.'

Graeme glared at the doctor. 'I'm all right, I promise. I want to go home now, please. Let me go home now.'

The doctor stared at Graeme. Long seconds passed.

'I can go home now, can't I?' Graeme smiled.

'You . . . can . . . go . . . home . . . now . . .' the doctor said at last.

Graeme smiled. 'Thanks a lot. I told you there was nothing wrong with me.'

'Who found me, Mum?' Graeme asked.

His mum honked her car horn at the man who had just cut across her lane.

'I hate driving at night,' she muttered. 'Pardon, dear?'

'Who found me?'

'Mrs Gowers. She's your French teacher, isn't she?' Mum drew to a stop as the traffic lights before her turned red.

Graeme nodded. 'Was there anyone else around at the time?'

'Not that Mrs Gowers mentioned. Why?'

'I just wondered.'

A light-coloured car came roaring up beside them before screeching to a loud, intimidating halt.

'Moron!' Graeme's mum hissed, casting a derisory glance in the other driver's direction.

The driver was Mrs Gowers. She smiled at Graeme. He didn't smile back.

'Mum, it's Mrs Gowers,' Graeme said, softly.

'Well, she should know better.' Graeme's mum tapped impatiently on her steering wheel as she waited.

The lights changed to show amber as well as red. With a screech even louder than before the other car sped away, even though the filter light was still against them.

'Really!' Graeme's mum shook her head as she released the handbrake. 'She's going to cause an accident before the night is out if she carries on like that.'

'Maybe she's got someone else to save.' Graeme stared after the car, now almost out of sight as it sped around a corner. 'I hope she does have an accident,' he muttered.

Graeme's mum turned to him, her gaze sharp. 'Graeme . . .'

'Sorry. I didn't mean it,' Graeme said quickly.

'Well, don't go saying things like that – even as a joke. Evil thoughts turn into evil deeds and they may fly out to do your bidding but sooner or later they come home to roost. Evil rebounds.'

Graeme sighed. 'It's only words.'

'*Only*! Graeme, if someone punches you, the pain lasts only a little while and then it's finished. But if someone says something horrible to you, believe me the pain lasts a lot longer. Sometimes the pain can last you all your life. *Only* indeed!'

Graeme looked out of the windscreen. He thought of Jude and the others and their spiteful taunts. Yes, he would remember them. For a *very* long time.

'Why don't you like your teacher?' Mum frowned.

'No reason.'

'It's not like you to dislike someone for no reason.'

'Please, Mum. Can we just drop it?'

'But your . . .' At Graeme's pleading look, she reluctantly let it go.

Graeme turned to stare out of the window. It wasn't fair. It just wasn't fair. He was being picked on because his skin colour was different to that of his tormentors. And as for Mrs Gowers – was that the best he could expect from grown-ups? Would they always look the other way and not get involved?

They turned the same corner as Mrs Gowers and went up the steep hill which became a ski-slope in the winter when ice and snow were on the ground.

'She's crashed into the greengrocer's window,' Graeme announced.

'Who's crashed . . . ?'

Mum's car cruised over the brow of the hill. There, at the foot of the hill, was the light-coloured car, its bonnet squashed up like an accordion. There were people all around it, shouting and yelling, with more running up.

'Oh my God!' Graeme's mum drove down to the bottom of the hill and pulled over, stopping the car.

'Why are you stopping?'

'I might be able to help,' his mum snapped, getting out of the car.

Graeme refused to budge. He sat in the car with his arms folded across his chest.

After a few moments, his mum walked back.

'What's going on?' Graeme asked.

'It's Mrs Gowers. She's unconscious but at least she's still alive. Someone's phoned for an ambulance.'

'What happened?'

Graeme's mum looked at him strangely. 'Mrs Gowers spun down the hill and careered straight into the greengrocer's window. It's lucky that no one was in the way.'

Graeme raised a hand to his suddenly throbbing temples. His mum started up the engine. She turned to him, her forehead creased, her eyes narrowed.

'How did you know she'd crashed into the greengrocer's?' she asked quietly.

'I saw her.'

The creases in his mum's forehead became more pronounced. 'You couldn't have. You said she'd crashed *before* we came over the hill.'

'No, I didn't. You've got it wrong.'

Graeme watched the people around the crumpled car, before wearily closing his eyes. His head was pounding as he replayed the crash scene over and over again. Mrs Gowers whizzing over the top of the hill . . . hitting the brakes to control her speed only to find they didn't work . . . her speed building up and up . . . the steering wheel locking up on her . . . fighting for control of her car which at each terrifying moment threatened to be wrenched away . . . the final spin as she lost the fight . . . and the fear within as she realised, horrified, what was about to happen . . . Mrs Gowers' chest hitting the steering wheel . . . her head whipping forward with the impact, whipping backwards as the bones in her neck cracked . . . sudden pain . . . sudden darkness . . .

'Let's get you home. We can't do any more here.' Graeme's mum's voice brought him out of his reverie.

Graeme took one last look at the wreckage, aware that what he had enjoyed fantasising about as Mrs Gowers sped away from them at the lights had actually happened.

As Graeme walked to school the next day, for the first time in ages he was actually looking forward to getting there. He was a bit late – his mother had insisted on fussing around him.

He turned the corner and saw them immediately. The bully boys with Jude out in front – as always. There was no one else around. Graeme stopped walking for a moment.

I'm not afraid of you, he thought, smiling inwardly. He always thought that whenever the bully boys were near him, but before it had been false bravado. Now, for the first time he really meant it. He carried on walking until he was only feet away from Jude and the rest.

'You better not have told anyone about us,' Lucas hissed as Graeme drew close.

Graeme didn't reply.

'He wouldn't do that,' Jude sneered. 'He's too much of a coward. Cannibal . . . Cannibal . . . CANNIBAL . . .'

Now all the boys joined in the chant.

'CANNIBAL . . . CANNIBAL . . .'

Graeme regarded each of the four boys in turn before turning his full attention to Jude whose eyes widened as he stared at Graeme.

And still Graeme said nothing.

Slowly, tortuously, Jude raised his arm. It trembled as if it was fighting to stay at his side. The litany Jude had been chanting choked off and died on his lips. Nervously, the others stopped chanting too.

Higher and higher rose Jude's arm. There could have been no one else in the world – just Graeme and Jude. They were fighting their last battle – a battle of wills.

Still trembling, Jude's arm moved towards his own mouth. His face took on a look of anguished horror as he glanced down at his arm then back at Graeme. Jude opened his mouth, placing his forearm against his teeth. His eyes stared at Graeme, with terror, with understanding. Jude chomped down hard onto his own arm. Blood spurted as Jude raised his arm again. His friends stared in horror as he bit into his own flesh for a second time. Matthew sprang into action, grabbing his friend's hand as he tried to pull it away from his mouth. Jude's face was set in a severe grimace as something forced him to chew on his own flesh.

Lucas vomited onto his shoes. Blood poured from the jagged wounds in Jude's arm. Jude's eyes glazed over. Graeme could see passers-by running up.

'Who's the cannibal now?' Graeme smiled at Jude.

Jude fell to his knees, his eyes still on Graeme before he pitched forward, unconscious. Graeme grinned at the other bully boys.

'Who's the cannibal now?' he repeated.

Graeme turned his back on them and walked into school. Today was going to be a good day.

Words Last Forever

Dear Robert,

I'm really sorry about doing it this way, but every time I try to talk to you, I just don't seem to be able to get the words out. That's why I finally plumped for this letter – which is something I always swore I'd never, ever do. But I had to. You see, the trouble is, I feel things too deeply. I always have done. That's why it's so hard for me to say no or to hurt someone. And I don't want to hurt you – God knows I don't. I like you. I really do.

It's just that, I don't want to go out with you any more. There, I've said it. I want you to know, I really do like you and I hope we can still be friends. I'd hate to lose your friendship. But I do feel it would be better if we stopped going out. It would solve all kinds of problems – for both of us. Don't you agree? Please don't think I'm being cowardly about this. I'm not. But you and I together, it causes so many – what's the word I'm looking for? – complications.

Take last Saturday, for instance. An ordinary, everyday trip to the cinema turned into . . . well, turned into an ordeal. I'd be lying if I said otherwise. We were stared and pointed at and I heard the people in the queue behind us making really nasty comments. I know you said we should just ignore them, and I did try – but I couldn't.

Words hurt. It's that simple.

Words stick and implant themselves and become part of you as physical pain never can. The pain from a punch or a slap fades and disappears eventually. Words last for ever. I'm not putting this very well. Robert, I guess what I'm trying to say is, I'm just not used to it. I thought I could handle all the attention the two of us together would provoke, but yesterday evening was the final straw. Now I realise that I was just lying to myself and being unfair to you.

I'm sure that once you've had a chance to sit down and think about it, you'll see I'm right.

So take care of yourself and I wish you only good things.

Yours in friendship,
Penny

Dear Penny,
This is the third letter I've written to you. I had to tear up the other two as soon as I'd finished them before the words burnt through the paper they were written on. If you want to stop going out with me because you've gone off me or because I have a bad case of body odour or swamp breath, then that's one thing. But to stop going out with me because of what other people do and say – that's something else entirely.

I like you. I mean, I *really* like you. I wouldn't have asked you out otherwise. You say you feel things deeply? Well, so do I. But I see your deep feelings don't extend in my direction. Please, Penny, don't do this. We're perfect for each other. I've never felt so comfortable with any other girl as I do with you. I can talk to you about anything. I don't have to put on a show or try and second guess you all the time. I don't want to lose that.

Can we meet up at our restaurant on Saturday? Say, eight o'clock? I think we should talk about this face to face.

Take care,
Robert

Dear Robert,

Can't we just be civilised about this and call it a day? I don't want to go out with you any more. I don't know how I can say it plainer that that. I don't understand why you can't see that this is for the best.

You say you feel comfortable with me? Well, I showed this letter to Gina and she agreed with me. The reason you feel comfortable with me is because you feel superior to me. I don't mean that in a nasty way. I'm not saying that you *deliberately* look down on me. But you don't see me as your equal. I know that in your own way you do like me – but why? Gina says it's because I'm not a threat. She says that you reckon no other boy could ever take me away from you. No other boy would ever want to.

Well, to be honest, I resent that. I'm not a charity case. I don't want you to go out with me because you feel sorry for me. So it's best if we just forget about going out together.

Please don't make this any harder than it has to be.

Penny

Dear Penny,

I couldn't believe my eyes when I read your last letter. How dare you say that to me? I thought you knew me a lot better than that. It just shows how wrong one man can be. Your sister opens her mouth and spouts any old load of rubbish and you instantly believe her. Answer me this – how on earth can your poisonous sister know what's going on in my head? I asked you out because I liked you. I wanted to be with you because I liked you. That was all there was to it. Nothing more, nothing less.

We both know what you're doing now. You're just trying to find excuses for not going out with me. You're clutching at any straw your sister throws at you. And I'll tell you why. Because you *are* a coward. You were wrong about that one as well. So what if people look and stare and point? That's their lookout, not ours. After the first couple of days of being with you, I didn't even notice – and that's the truth. You obviously did. You say you feel things deeply. I know that. What I didn't realise was that you allowed strangers to dictate how you should feel. I learnt a long time ago that you can't please everyone and if you try, you end up pleasing no one. So the only thing to do is please yourself. You're so busy trying to please your sister and your family, and Joe Bloggs who passes you on the street, that you and I have got lost somewhere in amongst all those people.

Penny, I still want to go out with you. I still care for you very, very much. I'm hoping that now you'll listen to me – and yourself. And no more letter writing please. Just phone me so we can talk about this, if not face to face than at least voice to voice.

All my love,
Robert

Robert,
For goodness sake! Can't you take no for an answer? I don't want to go out with you any more. Is that so hard for your humungous ego to comprehend? We're just not right for each other. Why can't you accept that so that we can both move on? I showed Gina your letter and d'you know what she said? I told you so – that's what she said. She warned me from the time I started going out with you that we weren't right together and that the day would come when I would regret ever saying yes to you – and she wasn't wrong. She warned me how everyone would laugh at us – at me especially. I only wish I'd listened to her a lot earlier than I did.

I'm not going to write another letter. This is my last one. I see no point in dragging this out. It just makes it more painful for both of us. It's time to move on. If you can't – or won't – then that's up to you. As far as I'm concerned, you and I are an old book that I've closed. I have no intention of opening it again.

Penny

Dear Penny,

Please don't think that this is a begging letter with me pleading for you to go back out with me. I realise that you've made up your mind and that's that. You've made a mistake – and that's not my ego talking. Or rather that's not *just* my ego talking. You and I could have gone a lot further and been so much happier if you'd only given us a chance – but as you said, that's over now. An old book.

But let me say this. Maybe when you've finished cursing me and have had a chance to calm down and think about it, you'll begin to see the truth in what I'm saying.

Watch out for your sister. Gina's been poisoning your mind against the very thought of the two of us together from the very beginning. And I'll tell you why as well. She's a bigot. It wasn't some mythical man or woman in the street that was sneering at us – it was your sister. She's the one who couldn't bear to see us together. And she's the one who's succeeded in splitting us up. No, I take that back. She couldn't have done it if you hadn't let her.

I bet I can guess exactly what your sister thought the first time she saw us together.

'Oh my God! What's my sister doing with someone like *him?*'

And shall I tell you something else, Penny? Your sister is jealous of you. I can see your expression as you read that bit. I can just imagine the look of scorn and disbelief on your face, but it's true. Gina knows that if you gave yourself a chance you'd be much better than her in all the things that count. She's the one who keeps telling you that you can't do this, you shouldn't do that, you mustn't do whatever. She's the one holding you back by constantly being negative about everything you try to do and be. D'you remember when I tried to persuade you to come on holiday with my family? It was perfectly innocent and above board – my parents wouldn't allow anything else – and you almost said yes. But Gina talked you out of it.

'Penny, think of the two of you on holiday together. It just wouldn't work. You'd stick out like a hammered thumb. You'd spoil the holiday for everyone. You certainly wouldn't have a good time.'

Gina went on and on. I can still hear her, like a dripping tap. On and on and on. Until you gave in. Just as you always give in and do everything she says. She keeps telling you that you shouldn't draw attention to yourself. Well, why the hell not? Why should you try to blend in and be the same as everyone else? Is that really what you want for the rest of your life?

When the two of us went anywhere together, I was always so proud of you – your good looks, your beautiful smile. But you'd rather believe your sister's lies.

You'll have to forgive me if this letter sounds bitter, but I guess it is. I suppose it won't make much difference if I tell you this now but I will anyway. I want you to know something. I love you. All those times I kissed you and told you that I really liked you, inside I was saying I loved you. I'm sorry I never said it out loud. Maybe it would've made a difference. Maybe it wouldn't have made any difference at all. I guess we'll never know.

Anyway, take care of yourself and don't let Gina drag you down.

All my love,
Robert

Robert,
I know I said I wouldn't write to you again, but I just had to say this. If you think that you can get back with me by

slagging off my sister, then you're deranged. I don't care if I never see you again.

Penny

Dear Robert,

How are you? I guess you're surprised to get a letter from me, especially after all this time and the last letter I wrote to you. I'm sorry about that. I've wanted to phone you and tell you how sorry I am about my last letter so many times, but I could never find the right words.

I was so happy to see you on Saturday. You looked very well. Even more great-looking than I remembered! I can't tell you how much I've missed you. The last eight months have crawled by. You were right of course. I was listening to everyone except myself. I still can't believe I could've got things so wrong.

Gina and I don't really talk much these days. A couple of months ago we were going for a meal when, across the street, Gina spotted a couple just like you and me.

'Look at that!' she said, shaking her head with disapproval.

Only then did she remember that she was with me instead of one of her other friends. I don't know which one of us was more shocked. She looked at me ruefully and we both laughed it off, but . . .

But.

I took out all your letters after that and read them and re-read them. It was as if I was just waking up. I can't believe I was so *stupid*. I look at Gina now, and the way she felt about you and me is so obvious. I can read her every expression like one of those neon signs at Piccadilly Circus. Why couldn't I see it before?

Robert, I want to say I'm sorry. I'd like to say it face to face. Maybe we can meet up – any time, any place, anywhere. Just say the word.

Yours, Penny

Dear Robert,

I'm not sure if you got my last letter. Although I didn't hear from you, I'm going to assume you did. I suppose I shouldn't really be surprised that you're still angry with me. I deserve it. But I know you're not one to hold a grudge.

That girl I saw you laughing with – is she your new girlfriend? I hope she isn't. There, I've said it. I'd really love to meet up with you again. What I mean is, I'd like to go out with you again.

I'm so sorry about the way I acted and the way I treated you. You deserved better than that. I'm sorry about a lot of things. I keep seeing Gina's face when we saw that couple like you and me. I still hear the words she said like Big Ben pealing in my head.

I know there are plenty of people out there who can't stand the thought of someone disabled going out with someone who isn't – but I never expected my sister to be one of them. You're one of the few people who noticed me first rather than my wheelchair. It's just a shame I didn't realise that eight months ago. Do write or phone or come and see me, Robert. I really would love to see you again. If that girl isn't your girlfriend then maybe we can pick up where we left off? Except I'd be different. I promise you, I won't use my wheelchair as an excuse or as a way of keeping you at arm's length.

Yours for ever,
Penny

Dear Robert,

Don't worry, I'm not going to keep pestering you with letters. I wish I'd broken up with you face to face or over the phone. Writing it down was a big mistake on my part, wasn't it? If I'd told you I didn't want to go out with you any more, the words would've become hazy and blurred around the edges after all this time. Writing it all down has

52

given you a permanently clear and sharp record of what I said. Do you re-read my letters at all? Do they still hurt as much? Maybe they just make you angry. Is that why you haven't contacted me? Maybe in your shoes I'd do the same thing.

I look at my wheelchair now and I hate it – more than I ever did before. It's a constant reminder of how I let it and my sister and a million silly things break us up. You'll never know how much I regret that.

Robert, I wish you the best of everything. Please, *please* do keep in touch. I'd love for us to be friends at least. Maybe you feel that's asking too much. I hope not. I know it's over between us as far as being an item is concerned, but I don't want to lose you completely.

Take care of yourself.

Ignore the smudges on the page.

Love,

Penny

Dear Penny,

Can we meet up on Friday evening? We could go to our usual restaurant. We have a lot to talk about. A lot to sort out.

All my love,

Robert

Dear Robert,

Of course we can meet up. I can't wait.

Yours for ever,

Penny

Behind the Mask

Perce didn't know what attracted him to the girl in the mask. Maybe it was the mask itself; shaped like a diving swallow with wide cat-eyed slits cut in the swallow's wings for the eyes. The swallow's tail and wings were edged with what looked like tiny, sparkling green emeralds which caught the light and dazzled the viewer. Maybe it was the girl's dress, of Grecian style and the same light emerald green as the mask edging.

Or maybe it was what he saw behind the mask, in her warm, mahogany brown eyes, laughing . . . at him? With him? Perce wasn't sure.

He'd been about to leave. The fancy dress party had failed to ignite and although a few people were dancing, most were standing around in small groups trying to make themselves heard over the relentlessly loud music.

Except for her.

She stood alone, watching him, watching all of them with that strange, slight smile on her lips. Taking a deep breath, Perce arrowed straight across the dance floor towards her. He wanted to get to her before another guy saw her. He was intrigued. Her eyes seemed to speak to him, to reflect her every thought. Perce noticed with satisfaction that the mystery girl watched as he crossed the suddenly crowded room. She smiled. With encouragement? With amusement? He couldn't tell.

She's probably laughing at this ridiculous costume, Perce thought sourly.

Why had he let himself be persuaded into wearing a musketeer's outfit? He'd never felt so foolish.

But faint heart and all that, Perce told himself, battling on. Undeterred he at last stood before her. And all the things he'd anticipated saying to her flew from his head and out the window.

'Hello, Perce,' the girl said.

'I see you know my name,' he groaned.

His name was the bane of his life. How he loathed it! And not even to himself did he admit what Perce was short for. He rued the perils of having a romantic mother.

'I asked about you,' the girl smiled.

Perce grinned. 'Why?' He thought he already knew the answer.

The girl shrugged delicately. 'I thought you looked . . . interesting. More interesting than most of the boys here.'

'It's kind of you to say so.'

The girl shook her head. 'I'm never kind.'

A shiver of anticipation trickled down Perce's spine. 'What's your name?' Perce asked.

She seemed to consider his question very carefully. 'My name? My name is . . . no! You guess it!'

'Like Rumpelstiltskin?' Perce laughed.

'I'll make it easy for you,' the mystery girl said carefully. 'My name begins with M.'

'Will you dance with me whilst I try to guess it?' Perce asked hopefully.

'Of course. I'm not going to let you out of my sight until you guess it correctly,' the girl smiled.

But there was something in her voice, something indefinable, something deep and calculating that made Perce wary for the first time.

'Who are you?'

'That's for you to find out,' the girl smiled again, taking his hand. 'I thought you were going to dance with me.'

'Let me see your face,' Perce said.

'Not yet,' the girl replied. 'Later – when you're ready, but not yet.'

'I don't understand. I'm ready to see your face now,' Perce argued.

'Not until you guess my name,' the girl replied firmly, leading Perce onto the dance floor.

A new song began. The girl started to dance, her movements liquid and sensual and somehow Perce kept up with her. It was as if her dance spirit had somehow captured him as well. He knew they looked good. He knew he had never danced better. All eyes were on them as they moved together.

But a strange thing was happening. As Perce danced, the music slowly grew louder and wilder, until his head was spinning. Then the music blended with the background hum, but still they danced. And before him was the mystery girl, smiling at him . . . laughing at him as she spun him around and around and around. Perce began to feel dizzy, nauseous. He wanted to stop dancing but the girl held his hands tightly and whirled him and he couldn't pull free. He tried to speak, to stop her, but the words spun out of his mouth and away from him without making sense. And still the music continued.

'Guess,' the girl ordered.

'What?' Perce gasped, trying to catch his breath.

'What's my name? Guess.'

'Maria.'

'No.'

'Mary.'

'No.'

'I . . . I must stop . . .'

'Guess,' the mystery girl demanded.

'Marsha . . .'

'No.'

'Please . . . I must stop.'

'Guess my name.'

Perce breathed out name after name after name and the music got louder and louder and wilder and wilder until everything around him was a rushing blur – except for the mystery girl.

'Maureen; Margaret; Mildred . . .'

'No, no, no,' the girl laughed.

Perce didn't know which was spinning faster now – the blood in his body or the room around him.

'Guess.'

Perce went through every girl's name beginning with M that he could think of, but to each guess the girl laughed delightedly and screamed, 'No.'

'I . . . I can't think of . . . of any more. Let me stop . . .' Perce could hardly get the words out. His lungs gasped frantically for air, his blood was roaring inside him. Another few moments and he would collapse.

'STOP!'

Abruptly the music stopped.

'Are you all right, Perce?' The girl's eyes were glinting.

Perce looked around, breathing deeply, frantically, as he fought to regain his breath. No one was taking any notice of him. Didn't they hear him shout for help?

'Are you all right, Perce? Is something wrong?'

'You . . . you . . .'

'Yes?' prompted the girl.

Perce blinked heavily as his lungs filled and his heart slowed. 'What just happened?' Perce asked.

The girl frowned. 'We were dancing and you were trying to guess my name. Then you suddenly stood still and started staring at me.'

'I did?'

The girl nodded. Perce ran his fingers through his already tousled hair. He looked around again, searching for a sign on someone's face that they knew what he'd just been through – but there was nothing. He felt sick.

'I . . . I need some air. I'll go outside for a while.'

'Shall I come with you?' she asked lightly.

Perce looked at her. Everyone else faded away. Perce felt as if he was at a crossroads, as if the answer to the mystery girl's question was vital. Perce shook his head to clear it. Now he was being fanciful!

'Don't you want me to accompany you?'

'No . . . I mean, yes, yes, please do.'

The girl linked her arm with his. 'Let's go this way, through the dining-room and the kitchen rather than fight our way back across the dance floor.'

'But what about the girl whose party this is? She might not like us traipsing through her other rooms,' Perce said doubtfully.

'She won't mind.'

'You don't know that.'

'Yes, I do, 'cause you're talking to her,' she laughed.

Perce frowned at her. 'But I thought this was the party of some girl called Emma?'

'M, not Emma. Everyone assumes that M is short for Emma but it's not. It stands for the letter M. Very few people know my real name. And I'm still waiting for you to guess it.'

M led the way through the dining-room and kitchen and down some stone steps to the back garden – if you could call it that. To Perce, it was so big, it looked more like a park! The moon was full and high, bathing the house and the grounds beyond in a cold, silver light. As yet the night air was warm and smelt of freesias and roses and a faint hint of orange blossom. Perce looked out over the vast lawn before him. There were flowers everywhere. Hedges broke up the huge expanse of lawn, and far across the lawn he saw what seemed to be silvery lights glinting. He sensed rather than saw that M was watching him.

'I hope you don't think I'm gatecrashing,' Perce said, after an uncomfortable silence on his part. 'Nichelle invited me. She said you wouldn't mind.'

'And she was right. I fact I told her to invite you,' M soothed. 'Come on, let's walk down to the lake.'

'There's a lake? Wow! This is some house!' Perce whistled.

'I like it!' M smiled.

Perce realised that the dull silvery glint he could see across the lawn had to be a part of the lake.

'So, where're your mum and dad?' Perce asked.

'Gone,' M replied simply.

What did that mean? Gone for the night? Gone on holiday? Gone for good? He didn't push it.

A soft breeze began to blow. M pulled the hairpins out of her hair until it fell free from its formal Grecian style, cascading down her back. She shook her head and laughed.

'I prefer my hair loose and free.'

'It looks better that way.'

'I think so.'

They walked across the vast lawn towards the lake. The wind was beginning to pick up now. It snatched at M's hair and tossed it all over her head. They rounded a high hedge which partially hid the lake from the house. Perce gasped. He had never seen so many statues in one place. They were all around the lake shore and beyond.

'Where did you get all these statues?' Perce asked curiously.

'I made them,' M said.

There was no pride or modesty in her voice. She was merely stating a fact.

'You made them? I'm impressed,' Perce said, taking another look around. 'Do you mind if I take a closer look?'

'Be my guest. This is where I come when I want to be alone with my thoughts,' M said softly. 'And I like to have all my men around me.'

'All your men?' Perce queried.

'Each of the statues is of a man,' M replied.

For the first time Perce saw that M was right. There were statues of men sitting, standing, leaning against other statues, touching other statues, running, walking. Statues of men laughing, crying, raging, hiding their heads behind their hands. Statues of surprised men, disbelieving men, amazed men – and all in a variety of dress. Mostly contemporary but some were dressed in period costume from across the centuries.

All at once, all the emotions, all the attitudes, overwhelmed Perce so that he had to look away. He turned to M. She was real and vivid. She was just what he needed to calm his imagination, which seemed to be working overtime tonight.

Perce looked back at the house. They were now too far away from it to hear the music, and the lights in the house were just tiny, candleflame-yellow sparks through the hedge. Perce turned his head to look out across the lake. He felt strange; giddy and dizzy again, only this time he and M were standing still and the rest of the world was spinning.

The wind was howling around them now.

Perce shivered. He began to feel distinctly uneasy. The water in the lake jumped and splashed in time to the wind's harsh whistling.

Perce looked around, his sense of unease growing. Then he noticed none of the statues were set on a plinth. They were all free standing, on their own legs. He walked over to the statue nearest him. He reached out to touch the modern jacket of the sculpture. Stone hard, stone cold. Perce frowned as he looked into the man's face. The expression was bewilderment. The attention to detail really was amazing.

'How do you get them to stand up without a base?'

'Guess my name and then I'll tell you.'

And the wind grew fiercer.

All at once a peculiar thought struck Perce. Icy fingers began to tap up and down his spine.

'Your name . . .' He turned his head slowly, 'Your name is . . .'

M had taken off her mask. Her whole face was alive and glowing with joy and laughter.

'I knew you'd get it,' she said happily.

Then the wind died. Not a murmur, not a whisper. But still M's hair writhed and slithered around her head.

'Medusa . . .'

It was the last word Perce ever said.

'Congratulations, Perce! Or would you rather I called you by your full name? And it's such a romantic name. A name that always brings out the best in me. Well, that's another Perseus for the collection.' Medusa's laugh tinkled like a small bell in the still, evening air.

And she ran up across the lawn and up the stone steps to rejoin the party.

Deeply

I feel things deeply – too deeply. That's always been my problem. I love too much. And when someone lets me down, I hurt too much. I know it, and yet I don't seem to be able to do anything about it.

Take my good friend, Caroline. She let me down badly – and yet I'd forgiven her. And here I was, keeping her company when, if I had any sense, I'd be doing something a lot more interesting, like cutting my toenails.

'I thought we were friends. I thought we were best friends,' Caroline complained.

I sighed. Caroline was at it again. Whinge, whine, moan, gripe! These days that was all she ever did.

'We are best friends.'

'I don't believe you, Helen . . .'

I sighed again. Sometimes Caroline reminded me of a small, yapping dog, snapping at my heels. She was my age – sixteen – with conker-coloured hair and huge, laughing eyes that made her face come alive. Only she hadn't done much laughing of late – only complaining. Why? I was the one who'd been hurt. I was the one who'd been betrayed by her. Yes, I had forgiven her . . . but I hadn't forgotten. Nor would I ever forget.

'We are best friends. We have been since we were seven.' I tried to placate her.

'Then why are you going out with him?' Caroline continued.

I took a deep breath, trying to smother the angry impatience rising up in me. I didn't have to be here, I really didn't.

'Caroline, give me a break. Luke is just a friend. He makes me laugh and we've been to the cinema together a few times. That's it. End of story. No big deal. And besides, you're the one who went out with Luke first. You knew I liked him but you went out with him anyway. And you're the one who didn't have any time for me after you started going out with him – remember?'

'Yeah, and you took care of that,' Caroline said bitterly.

'What was I supposed to do?' Even now I couldn't keep the bitterness out of my voice. 'Suddenly it was you and Luke, and I didn't exist any more.'

'And now you've taken over where I left off.'

'Look, I've had enough of this. I'm going home.' I stood up.

Caroline grabbed my arm. 'No, don't. I'm sorry. I'll shut up about Luke.'

I didn't sit down again. Truth to tell, I wanted to go home. Caroline was no fun any more.

I looked around, taking in the tall horse chestnut trees, their leaves green hands miming to each other in the gentle breeze. It was a slow, sleepy, summer evening. The sun was low in the red-orange sky and somewhere nearby a solitary bird was chirping. It was my favourite time of day.

'So what did you do today?' Caroline asked, shuffling to sit properly on the brick wall which surrounded her home.

I gave in and sat down beside her. 'Not much. Went to school. Went home. Came here to see you.'

I could see that that pleased Caroline. A smile lit her face. Then the smile faded.

'You really like Luke, don't you?' Caroline asked, watching me.

I shrugged, then grinned sheepishly.

'I liked Luke,' Caroline said quietly. 'I was really stuck on him.'

'He liked you a lot, too. He still talks about you,' I told her, with a forced smile.

That really made her day. She beamed at me like a lighthouse. I sighed inwardly. Caroline was such hard work.

'So what have you been up to?' I asked, trying to disguise my lack of interest.

'I chatted to Mrs Silver. She's just moved in next to me.'

'What's she like?'

'Not bad for an oldie . . .' Caroline wittered on whilst I did my best to make the appropriate noises in the right places. Surprisingly it didn't take Caroline long to catch on to what I was doing.

'You're not listening to a single word I'm saying, are you?' she fumed.

'Of course I am,' I protested.

Caroline glared at me, her expression icy. 'I think you're really mean, Helen. I'm only here because of you . . .'

'Caroline, I don't mean to be unkind, but please don't start . . .' I didn't get any further.

'Don't start! I spend all day and all night here . . . in this place . . . I have no real friends, no one to talk to, no one to confide in – except you. You don't even come to see me every day as you promised me you would. And then, when you're here, you can't wait to get away . . .'

'I'm sorry. I just have a lot on my mind at the moment.'

'Yeah, but you can walk away from whatever is troubling you. I can't. I'm stuck here – thanks to you,' Caroline said tearfully. 'Go away, Helen. You know you want to. Go away and leave me alone.'

'Don't be like that, Caroline,' I said. 'I know it's my fault you're here but . . .'

'There are no "buts",' Caroline dismissed. 'You couldn't give a stuff about how I feel. All I ask you to do is visit me every evening – that's all. Even if it's only for five minutes. That's not too much to expect, is it?'

Not too much to expect . . .

I thought about what Caroline had said as I walked home. She was right. It was my fault she was stuck in that place. For the first time I thought about what it would be like to be Caroline with no one to really talk to. I wouldn't like it – not one little bit.

All right then, Caroline, I thought. I'll try harder. I really will. I'll see what I can do. Then you'll have to stop blaming me for everything bad that's ever happened to you.

As I walked home I wondered if I could get a friend to visit Caroline with me. Not Luke. Never Luke. But someone else. A mutual friend. It would be a bit tricky to manage but if I could pull it off then maybe Caroline wouldn't feel quite so isolated. Another wave of overwhelming guilt swept over me, but for a different reason. Even now, I couldn't bear the thought of Caroline and Luke together. After everything that'd happened I still felt . . . jealous. Another wave descended over me, and another. Her accident was my fault. And the way she made me feel – that was my fault too. So what could I do? Except blame myself and deep, deep down resent Caroline for the way she made me feel. All I knew was that I had to do something.

'Luke, do you still think about Caroline Fisher?'

'Yes of course. I was devastated when I heard about her accident . . .'

I nodded. It was Saturday afternoon and we were in our usual Saturday afternoon haunt – Pizza Perfection. If it wasn't for our group I reckoned the place would go out of business.

'What about Caroline?' Luke asked.

'Do you . . . did you like her?'

Luke shrugged, trying to look nonchalant. 'Yeah, she was all right. We got on well together. She was the same person all the time. I liked that.'

What did he mean by that? I let it pass.

'Why d'you ask?'

'I think about her – sometimes,' I replied.

'So do I – sometimes. I liked Caroline. She was a good laugh.'

'Helen, Caroline was your best friend,' Gina, another girl from our group said gently. 'It's only natural that you should think about her.'

'Yeah . . .' I nodded. I glanced down at my watch. 'Come on, Luke, we're going to miss the start of the film if we don't move. You did remember to bring the tickets, didn't you?'

Luke frowned at me. 'You've got the tickets.'

I pursed my lips, whilst the others around us started grinning. 'No, Luke, I gave the tickets to you three days ago.'

'No, you didn't,' Luke's frown deepened.

'Yes I did,' I said patiently. 'And you said you were going to put them on your bedside table so you wouldn't forget them.'

'Oh hell! Did I?'

Everyone around us was cracking up by now!

'Oh, Luke,' I sighed. 'I'm not going all the way to your house and back. I'll wait for you outside the cinema whilst you go back home for the tickets.'

I stood up and walked out of the restaurant. Luke had no choice but to follow me. I could tell he was behind me without having to look around. I also knew that our friends were watching. I must confess, it gave me a sense of . . . power – like a movie star.

'Actually, Luke,' I said, once we were alone outside, 'I've changed my mind. I will come back to your house with you if you like.'

My moment as a movie star was over. The scene for the benefit of our friends could be abandoned now that we were alone. I didn't want my friends to think that Luke had me wrapped around his little fingernail! Once a girl gets a rep for being a wet rag she can't get rid of it.

Luke gave me a strange look.

'Yeah, OK,' he shrugged at last. 'I'm sorry about the tickets, Helen. I was sure you had them.'

'It doesn't matter,' I smiled.

As if anything could ever matter except being with him.

We started walking along in silence. I kept glancing at Luke, unable to believe my luck. I was an item with the hunkiest boy in our school. Somewhere, somehow, I must have done something *right*! We ducked furtively into the alley by Mr Pen's newsagent's – he didn't like us using his alley as a short cut – and started walking along the canal. I love the canal. It's filthy-disgusting, but on a day like today the whole world was beautiful.

'Actually, I'm glad you decided to come with me,' Luke began slowly. 'I have something to tell you and I think . . . I think I should tell you sooner rather than later.'

'What is it?' I smiled up at him. He really was gorgeous. Blue-black skin and the darkest brown eyes I'd ever seen. And when he smiled . . . it was like star bursts and fireworks. When he kissed me . . . his lips were so soft, so gentle. I was crazy about him. I had been from the time he'd come to our school two years ago but it was a secret, like a blazing fire deep down inside me. I knew why Caroline had forgotten about me once she'd started going out with Luke. I'd have done the same thing. Well, at least Luke was mine – now that Caroline was out of the picture. I still couldn't feel sorry about that. I'd be a liar if I said otherwise.

'Helen . . . I don't know how to say this without just . . . saying it. So . . .' Luke took a deep breath, 'I don't . . . I don't want to . . . go out with you any more.'

I frowned, then smiled up at Luke, sure he was joking. 'What?'

'I don't want to go out with you any more.' Luke repeated the words without stumbling over them this time.

I stared up at him. My smile slowly faded. 'Why?' I asked, my throat tight.

'I just don't.'

'There must be a reason.'

Luke shrugged. 'I've thought and thought about it and I just think it would be better if we didn't go out together any more. We can still be friends though . . .'

'Is there someone else?'

'No. I just . . .'

'You're just tired of me,' I interrupted.

We stopped walking. I looked down at the brown-grey canal water, dull and dirty and disgusting.

'Helen, please try to understand. Be reasonable . . .'

'Reasonable?' The word burnt my mouth.

I stood still, staring into the canal. Luke stood next to me. I could sense his uncertainty. He wanted to go. He wanted to be as far away from me as possible. Inside I was choking, screaming. First Caroline, now Luke.

We stood in silence for a while.

'Don't get too close to the water, Luke. You can't swim, can you?'

'Not a stroke, but don't worry, I have no intention of getting anywhere near that lot!' Luke retorted, eyeing the murky, muddy water with distaste.

I looked around, my heart hurting. Hurting deeply.

It was so peaceful here – green and peaceful. But suddenly the world wasn't beautiful. My life was the canal. The canal was my life. Filthy-disgusting.

'Do you ever wonder what's in there? D'you ever wonder what goes on deep down in there?' I asked.

'No, I don't. And whatever is down there can stay down there as far as I'm concerned.'

Luke's voice grew stronger, more confident as he spoke. Now that we were off the embarrassing subject of him dumping me, he was happy to speak to me. All I could think of was that he was deserting me.

First Caroline, now Luke.

'Luke, did you tell any of your friends that you're dumping me?'

'I'm not dumping you,' Luke protested.

'Just answer the question, please.'

'I didn't tell them we were splitting up – no. I wanted to speak to you first. This is between you and me.'

'I see . . .' I said slowly.

Silence.

'Well . . . if that's how you really feel, then I guess . . . oh my . . . Look at that!' I pointed at the canal water.

'At what?' Luke's gaze followed my pointed finger.

'At that! At that! What is it?'

'What?' Luke moved forward a step and bent forward over the canal to take a closer look.

I took one last quick look around. Then I pushed him.

Luke did a somersault before landing in the water, his arms flailing. He went under immediately. Seconds passed before his head surfaced. He gasped and retched, spitting out the filthy canal water.

'Hel . . . Helen . . .' he gasped. His head went under again.

I looked around. This was the most dangerous part. If anyone should come by now . . .

Luke's head re-surfaced. He spat out more water, his arms slamming against the surface of the water, over and over.

'Helen . . . help . . .' he cried. 'I can't . . . I can't swim . . .'

'Yes, I know,' I whispered.

'For God's sake . . .' he screamed.

I took another look around. There was no one in sight.

'HELEN!'

Luke tipped his head back, fighting for air, fighting to clear the water. He didn't. He couldn't. He went under again – only this time he didn't reappear.

I watched for a while to make sure he wouldn't come up again. I could hardly risk that. That'd been my mistake when I pushed Caroline into the canal. I'd left too soon and someone else had found her. Luckily for me, Caroline died without regaining consciousness – otherwise I don't know what might have happened.

Nope, it looked like Luke had definitely gone down for good. I walked back to the cinema. I made a big show of checking my watch every couple of minutes whilst the queue of people behind me moved slowly into the cinema. Then I stormed back to Pizza Perfection.

'Is Luke in here?' I asked, furious.

'No. I thought you two were going to see a film?' Benji replied.

'So did I. I've been stood up. The film's started now,' I fumed.

I stayed in the restaurant with the rest of them until the evening. They didn't find Luke's body until four days afterwards, floating face down in the canal, all swollen and bloated. When they told me he'd been found, I cried and cried. For days I was inconsolable. It was as if a part of me had died too. I mean it. Luke was . . . Luke was my love. He'd always have a special place in my heart. I know that because I feel things so deeply.

'Hi, Caroline, how are you?' I smiled.

'I'm fine, Helen. And you?'

'Not bad,' I shrugged, 'not bad. Well, Luke, aren't you going to say hello?'

Luke turned his head away from me. His face was ashen, his eyes huge and staring.

He's looked better, I thought with distaste.

'I'm glad you're here, Luke. It's good to see you.'

He looked at me, then looked away.

'I know you're upset, but you'll get over it,' I smiled.

Honestly! What was I supposed to do? Luke had tried to leave me, desert me – just like Caroline. I had to do something . . .

Besides, Caroline wanted a friend to keep her company and if I couldn't have him, Luke was the ideal candidate.

He'll forgive me. He has to.

After all, apart from whinging Caroline and some boring old dears, who else has he got to talk to?

Rest in Peace

'General Shaw, I came as soon as I could.' Colonel Huenecke kicked the door shut behind her and marched over to General Sam Shaw's huge, imposing mahogany desk.

'Thank you, Colonel,' said General Shaw. 'Take a seat.'

'You said over the phone that you've found her?' the colonel queried, swamping the old-fashioned armchair she sat down in.

General Shaw pursed his lips, slowly swivelling his chair to the left, to the right.

'Before I tell you what I know,' he began, ' I want you to tell me everything you can about Sergeant Malone's last mission.'

'But sir, every second we wait . . .'

'I have my reasons – good reasons. Sergeant Malone isn't going anywhere – not for a while at least.' The general swung his chair through one hundred and eighty degrees to stare out of the huge window that made up one whole wall of his spacious office.

He still couldn't get used to the lime-green sky of Toxton, dominated by its one orange sun. It revolted him. How he hated it here.

He'd been brought in to play detective by the Alliance and he couldn't wait to clear up his current case and go home. He was old and tired and all he wanted to do was return to Earth with his wife. How he missed her. They had been married for less than a year. A secret ceremony on the tiny planet of Morgell, with only two Morgellians as witnesses and a Rygart MOC to marry them.

'I don't want any fuss, Sam,' Maure told him. 'And you know what a circus our wedding will turn into if the Alliance hear that the famous General Shaw is getting married.'

Sam secretly wanted a big fuss. He wanted to show her off to the whole galaxy. He wanted a wedding that would be talked about for decades. But Maure wasn't like that. Maure was quiet, deep. She hated fuss, she hated the thought of anyone pointing to her and saying, 'That's General Shaw's wife.'

'I'm not an appendage to you,' Maure had said stubbornly, when Sam tried to argue. 'I have my own interests, my own career and I'm not giving them up.'

'I never asked you to. But OK, we'll get married your way.'

'You'd like all the fuss and public ceremony though,' Maure sighed. 'I'm sorry, Sam, but I . . .'

'Listen, Maure. You're the most important thing in the world to me. I love you. I thought at my age I'd never say those words.'

'Your age! You're not in your dotage yet!' Maure scoffed and Sam loved her even more for it. Sam was more than twice her age.

'It's just that, by the time the marriage certificate gets through from Morgell to central records I'll have really established my career and then it won't matter who knows. We'll have our celebratory party then – I promise,' Maure said.

And Sam had agreed. If she'd told him to put a phaser to his temple and disintegrate his head he would've done it. What was the old Earth saying? There's no fool like an old fool!

'Sir . . . ? Sir?'

General Shaw turned back to the colonel. 'I'm sorry, soldier. It's been a long day.'

Colonel Huenecke gave an embarrassed smile. 'About Sergeant Malone, sir. The sergeant has already murdered three assignment officers. There's only General Pierre and myself left, sir, from the original assignment group.'

'And you're sure Sergeant Malone is responsible?' the general asked seriously, burying all other thoughts.

'The sergeant fits the profile,' the colonel nodded. 'There are two possibilities. We know for certain that Sergeant Malone was captured. So either the soldier has been brainwashed by the Toxtons or else blames us assignment officers for the fact that . . . well, sir, we believe the Toxtons used torture . . .'

'You know that for a fact?'

'Yes, sir. Our spy patrol pinpointed the sergeant in the Terra-wing of the Toxtons' camp. That's their torture centre. Very few humans come out of there alive.'

'And which theory do you believe?'

'Sir?'

'Do you believe the sergeant has been brainwashed or is this a desire for some kind of warped revenge?'

'I believe it's the latter, sir.'

'Why?'

'Why would the Toxtons want Major Parry, Colonel Daniels and Lieutenant Turner dead, sir? There are far more important people on this base – militarily and strategically speaking. There's no other explanation for the three deaths that have already occurred within the base, or for the near miss which happened to me yesterday,' replied Colonel Huenecke.

'I want you to tell me exactly what happened. A complete report. I want to know why Sergeant Malone would be after you.'

'But sir, couldn't this wait? Shouldn't we . . . ?' Colonel Huenecke shut up at the look on the general's face.

'Well it was like this, sir,' she had difficulty suppressing her impatience. 'It all began . . .'

Sergeant Malone marched into the office and stood to attention.

'At ease, soldier,' Colonel Huenecke said, gruffly.

Behind the rectangular table sat five brass necks – Colonel Huenecke, General Pierre, Colonel Daniels of the 11th, Major Parry and Lieutenant Turner.

'You have been chosen,' began General Pierre as the ranking officer, 'to infiltrate the Toxtons and bring back their plans for the invasion of this base.'

'Invasion?' queried Sergeant Malone, wide-eyed with shock.

'Invasion. We have intelligence which indicates that they plan to invade the base in an all-or-nothing attack, but we don't know when and we don't know where. Getting that information will be your mission.'

'I don't understand . . .'

'You'll be fully briefed before you leave. Thanks to previous reconnaissance teams we have a map of the ingress and egress points of the Toxton camp and guard movements on their perimeter. I cannot stress strongly enough the importance of your mission. I'm taking a gamble and assigning ninety-five percent of the garrison to the Maristoke west wall. It's the logical place for a Toxton attack and the easiest to breach since our last set-to with them. But it means that our east wall will be totally vulnerable. I think the Maristoke wall will be where they'll strike next but I need to know for certain and I need to know when.'

'When do I set off, sir?' Sergeant Malone asked.

'Tonight,' Colonel Daniels answered for the general.

'I see, sir.' Sergeant Malone swallowed hard.

'Your task is to get to the Toxtons' strategic base where they hold their plans and to record them. Then you're to report straight back here. No heroics.' Colonel Daniels continued, 'And just one more thing, soldier. If it looks like the Toxtons are closing in you mustn't let them take you alive.'

'I understand, sir,' the sergeant replied quietly.

'You know our plans, sergeant. We can't risk the Toxtons finding out that ninety-five percent of our garrison are protecting the Maristoke wall.' General Pierre took over. 'You'll be issued with a bredrillin ampoule. If you get caught, I trust you'll know what to do?'

'Yes, sir,' said the sergeant.

'Major Parry and Lieutenant Turner recommended you for this assignment, sergeant. Don't let them down,' said the general.

'I won't, sir.'

'And I was the one who brought their recommendation to the general, Sergeant Malone,' said Colonel Huenecke. 'I expect you to succeed. Is that understood?'

'Yes, sir.'

'Any questions, soldier?' asked General Pierre.

'No, sir.'

Which wasn't strictly true. She did have one question. Only one. Why me? But she was too well trained to give voice to her question. Besides, here at last was her chance to shine. With one last salute, Sergeant Malone turned sharply and marched out of the room.

The sun was just setting, turning the green sky that oak-leaf green colour Sergeant Malone could never get used to. She could see the Toxton settlement although she was still a good few kilometres away from it. She didn't dare get any closer until the sun had completely set. Twelve hours . . . she had twelve hours to get into the Toxton camp, find the information General Pierre wanted and get out again. Once again Sergeant Malone wondered why they had chosen her. She'd had a fairly undistinguished military career to date. Five years on the planet with the usual holidays and nothing this exciting or dangerous had ever been assigned to her. Sergeant Malone daydreamed that maybe the military had finally recognised her potential and were willing to give her a chance. But surely they would never assign such an inexperienced soldier as herself to such an important task as this. Yet, here she was . . .

Pride mingled with trepidation as Sergeant Malone edged forward on her stomach. Sparse plants and brush dug into her. The ground was hot and smelt sour – a smell that reminded Sergeant Malone of the limes to be found back on Earth.

Why did they choose me? Sergeant Malone couldn't get the question out of her head. She glanced down at the datapack on her wrist.

'Map. Current sector,' she hissed down to it. She had to be careful. There were sound-sensitive, recording mines as well as explosive mines all around her.

'Let's hope intelligence have got the mine configuration for this sector right. Otherwise this is going to be the fastest failed mission in history.'

She studied her datapack again. The map showed all the mines in the surrounding area by minute, blinking dots. Sergeant Malone slipped on her magnifocal glasses and studied the datapack. Working her way through the maze of mines and traps would be slow, laborious work. But it was that or get herself blown up or, worse still, captured. And the minutes were ticking away.

Three hours later Sergeant Malone breathed a huge sigh of relief. She was at the perimeter and if the intelligence she'd been given was correct, there should be a small gap in the perimeter defences just about where she was. A gap small enough for her to plant sensor deflectors so that the Toxton defence radar would pick up no breach in the perimeter wall. Setting the sensor deflectors, Sergeant Malone crawled through the gap on her stomach, her head down.

Using her magnifocal lenses, she again studied the map for this new sector.

'Guard details,' she whispered to the mechanism on her wrist.

The map details disappeared and the guard positions for her sector came on screen.

'Position of Toxton strategy base,' Sergeant Malone whispered.

'Come with us and we'll show you.'

Sergeant Malone's head snapped up, her hand to the phaser strapped to her hip.

'I wouldn't do that if I were you.'

She was surrounded. Toxtons were all around her.

Sergeant Malone froze. She felt physically sick. She could taste bitter failure. She hadn't even made it to the building which housed the Toxtons' plans. She had nothing to report, nothing to say to them back at base. She had failed. At least the Toxtons wouldn't take her alive.

But what a way to die . . .

Sergeant Malone bit into her right cheek, feeling the ampoule between her teeth. She bit harder, her whole body shaking. She felt the warm, sweet liquid from the ampoule mingle with blood from her cheek and rush over her tongue. She swallowed hard, full of regret but knowing she had no other choice.

'Get to your feet,' the Toxton directly in front of her ordered.

Sergeant Malone stood up slowly, wondering, terrified, how long the poison in the ampoule would take to work. Surely it should have been instantaneous? Would it be painful or would she feel nothing?

'I don't know who you've offended,' the lead Toxton laughed, 'but someone in your camp doesn't like you.

We've known your exact position from the time you set foot out of your base.'

Sergeant Malone stared at him. Then she gave a smile. For a brief moment there she had almost believed the Toxton. But the Toxton would soon be deprived of his entertainment.

'I see you don't believe me. What if I were to tell you that that ampoule you've just broken in your mouth contains a harmless relaxant? I had the real ampoule of bredrillin substituted for the one you have in your mouth, back at your base.'

Sergeant Malone stared at him.

'Surely you must be wondering why you're still alive?' said the Toxton. 'If the ampoule contained its proper contents, you would have been dead two seconds after you'd bitten into it.'

Sergeant Malone felt her stomach churn. The Toxton's face twisted into an even more severe grimace.

'We have a certain worker in your camp who's on our side. He told us all about your . . . impending arrival. Now you will tell us all about your mission.'

'Go to hell,' Sergeant Malone hissed. 'My name is Sergeant Malone, I'm a sergeant in the Alliance army and my service code is USE-4424-1M4-Malone. That's all you're going to get out of me.'

'We'll see,' the Toxton shrugged. 'We'll see.'

And Sergeant Malone was led away.

'That's all our surveillance radar picked up,' said Colonel Huenecke.

'Did you find out who the spy in our camp was?' General Shaw asked, facing the sky which was slowly turning from lime to olive green.

'We . . . we always knew who the spy was, sir.' Colonel Huenecke frowned. 'That was part of our overall plan.'

'Then I take it that there was more to this than just sending Sergeant Malone to get the data General Pierre said he wanted?' General Shaw turned to face the colonel.

Colonel Huenecke looked down at her highly polished shoes. For the first time she looked uncomfortable and ill at ease.

'The five assignment officers devised a plan, sir, called Operation Counter,' Colonel Huenecke began.

'Operation Counter?' General Shaw prompted when the colonel would say no more.

'It was top secret, sir.'

'I have full security clearance, soldier. If I'm to understand what's been going on here I need all the facts.' General Shaw tried to keep the impatience out of his voice.

'Well, sir . . .' the colonel said reluctantly. 'We thought . . . General Pierre thought that Operation Counter would be our chance to wipe out the Toxtons once and for all.'

'How?'

Colonel Huenecke took a deep breath before continuing. 'Operation Counter involved feeding false information to a likely subject and allowing that subject to fall into enemy hands.'

There was a long pause as General Shaw regarded the colonel.

'Let me get this straight,' said General Shaw at last. 'You gave Sergeant Malone false information and set her up with a harmless ampoule in her cheek, hoping that she'd get caught and tortured by the Toxtons, so that she could give them false information. Is that about right?'

'Yes, sir,' Colonel Huenecke said, grimly. 'But you must understand, the Toxtons had to be destroyed. Their last strike against us was successful – too successful. We suffered many casualties. Malone was expendable.'

'You checked her file?'

'Yes, sir. She had no living family. No close friends. She was a loner, sir, so she was ideal for the job. And her psychiatric evaluation seemed to indicate that she would crack easily under pressure.'

'I see . . . And the false information you wanted her to pass on to the Toxtons?' asked General Shaw, his back to the colonel as he looked out over the human camp.

'The Maristoke west wall, sir.'

'Of course.' The general nodded his head. 'I take it we wanted the Toxtons to strike anywhere but there?'

'We briefed Sergeant Malone that the weakest area in our garrison was the Kafnz East Wall, sir. That's where we were really going to concentrate our forces and wait for the Toxtons. The fact that the Toxtons haven't attacked us yet would seem to indicate that Sergeant Malone held out long enough to escape. And now she's after us.'

'Do you know what the Toxton mind machines do? Do you know they leave their victims helpless vegetables after they've been subjected to them for any length of time?' General Shaw swung around in his chair to directly face Colonel Huenecke.

'Yes, sir, but as I said, Sergeant Malone was deemed expendable.'

'I see. And the spy in the camp?'

'He was disposed of, sir, once the sergeant was under way. We thought we'd have no further use for him.'

'I see,' the General breathed deeply. 'Only your plan didn't work. Sergeant Malone escaped.'

Colonel Huenecke looked away from the general then quickly back.

'Yes, sir. We all thought she'd break long before she did. But, sir, guts and courage like that don't show up on the assessment reports. Sergeant Malone must have had a great will to live. She escaped – and now she's found out about what we did to her – why we sent her to the Toxton camp . . .'

'And that's why she's killing each of you? It makes sense,' said General Shaw. 'Yes, it does make sense.'

'Which is why you must tell me where she is, sir,' Colonel Huenecke said eagerly. 'Then I can have her kept under close confinement before her trial and execution.'

'And you're convinced it is Sergeant Malone?' asked General Shaw.

'Who else could it be, sir?'

'How about her husband?'

The colonel stared at General Shaw. 'Her husband? She wasn't . . . married . . .'

'Yes she was. In fact, today would have been our six months anniversary.' General Shaw removed his phaser from his desk.

The colonel stared at the general, before springing out of her chair, horror-stricken. 'General Shaw . . .'

The general aimed his phaser and without another word fired at the colonel's heart. Colonel Huenecke clutched at her chest in agony before her body dropped like a stone to the floor.

'That's for you, Maure,' General Shaw whispered.

His wife was dead. Shot and killed whilst trying to escape from the Toxtons. He hadn't found her body yet – no one had – but he knew she was out there – somewhere. General Shaw had known the exact moment of her death even though he'd been halfway across the galaxy at the time. He'd known from the strange burning in his chest and the stinging of his eyes.

'Just one more, my darling,' General Shaw smiled sadly. 'I've left the biggest and best for last. General Pierre is next, my love – and then I'll find you and take you home. Then you can rest in peace.'

Music on the Bamboo Radio

By Martin Booth

If the enemy catch him, they'll kill him . . .

Nicholas Holford is smuggled to safety in China when Japan invades Hong Kong in 1941. Not knowing if his parents are alive or dead, he must pretend to be Chinese. If the enemy discovers he is European, he will not survive.

Then Nicholas joins the secret fight against the Japanese. He learns about explosives, but also about 'music on the bamboo radio' – smuggling information to prisoner-of-war camps. It is dangerous and deadly. But when only Nicholas can help, he chooses to take the risk . . .

Age 12+   ISBN: 0 435 12490 0

ALSO IN

Heinemann
New Windmills

Founding Editors: Anne and Ian Serraillier

Chinua Achebe Things Fall Apart
David Almond Skellig
Maya Angelou I Know Why the Caged Bird Sings
Margaret Atwood The Handmaid's Tale
Jane Austen Pride and Prejudice
J G Ballard Empire of the Sun
Stan Barstow Joby; A Kind of Loving
Nina Bawden Carrie's War; Devil by the Sea; Kept in the Dark; The Finding; Humbug
Lesley Beake A Cageful of Butterflies
Malorie Blackman Tell Me No Lies; Words Last Forever
Martin Booth Music on the Bamboo Radio
Ray Bradbury The Golden Apples of the Sun; The Illustrated Man
Betsy Byars The Midnight Fox; The Pinballs; The Not-Just-Anybody Family; The Eighteenth Emergency
Victor Canning The Runaways
Jane Leslie Conly Racso and the Rats of NIMH
Robert Cormier We All Fall Down
Roald Dahl Danny, The Champion of the World; The Wonderful Story of Henry Sugar; George's Marvellous Medicine; The BFG; The Witches; Boy; Going Solo; Matilda; My Year
Anita Desai The Village by the Sea
Charles Dickens A Christmas Carol; Great Expectations; Hard Times; Oliver Twist; A Charles Dickens Selection
Peter Dickinson Merlin Dreams
Berlie Doherty Granny was a Buffer Girl; Street Child
Roddy Doyle Paddy Clarke Ha Ha Ha
Anne Fine The Granny Project
Jamila Gavin The Wheel of Surya
Graham Greene The Third Man and The Fallen Idol; Brighton Rock
Thomas Hardy The Withered Arm and Other Wessex Tales
L P Hartley The Go-Between
Ernest Hemmingway The Old Man and the Sea; A Farewell to Arms
Frances Mary Hendry Chandra
Barry Hines A Kestrel For A Knave
Nigel Hinton Getting Free; Buddy; Buddy's Song; Out of the Darkness
Anne Holm I Am David

Janni Howker Badger on the Barge; The Nature of the Beast; Martin Farrell
Pete Johnson The Protectors
Jennifer Johnston Shadows on Our Skin
Geraldine Kaye Comfort Herself
Daniel Keyes Flowers for Algernon
Clive King Me and My Million
Dick King-Smith The Sheep-Pig
Elizabeth Laird Red Sky in the Morning; Kiss the Dust
D H Lawrence The Fox and The Virgin and the Gypsy; Selected Tales
George Layton The Swap
Harper Lee To Kill a Mockingbird
Julius Lester Basketball Game
C Day Lewis The Otterbury Incident
Joan Lingard Across the Barricades; The File on Fraulein Berg
Penelope Lively The Ghost of Thomas Kempe
Jack London The Call of the Wild; White Fang
Bernard MacLaverty Cal; The Best of Bernard Mac Laverty
Margaret Mahy The Haunting
Anthony Masters Wicked
James Vance Marshall Walkabout
Ian McEwan The Daydreamer; A Child in Time
Pat Moon The Spying Game
Michael Morpurgo My Friend Walter; The Wreck of the Zanzibar; The War of Jenkins' Ear; Why the Whales Came; Arthur, High King of Britain
Beverley Naidoo No Turning Back
Bill Naughton The Goalkeeper's Revenge
New Windmill A Charles Dickens Selection
New Windmill Book of Classic Short Stories
New Windmill Book of Fiction and Non-fiction: Taking Off!
New Windmill Book of Haunting Tales
New Windmill Book of Humorous Stories: Don't Make Me Laugh
New Windmill Book of Nineteenth Century Short Stories
New Windmill Book of Non-fiction: Get Real!
New Windmill Book of Non-fiction: Real Lives, Real Times
New Windmill Book of Scottish Short Stories
New Windmill Book of Short Stories: Fast and Curious
New Windmill Book of Short Stories: Tales with a Twist

How many have you read?